Buffy the Vampire Slayer™

FOOD CHAIN

Buffy the Vampire Slayer

Food Chain

based on the television series created by
JOSS WHEDON

featuring CHRISTOPHER GOLDEN, CHRISTIAN ZANIER,
CLIFF RICHARDS, TOM SNIEGOSKI, JASON MINOR,
TOM FASSBENDER, JIM PASCOE,
CHYNNA CLUGSTON-MAJOR, RYAN SOOK, JAMIE S. RICH,
and DOUG PETRIE

with GUY MAJOR, ANDY OWENS, JOE PIMENTEL,
CURTIS P. ARNOLD, LEE LOUGHRIDGE, MARVIN MARIANO,
DRAXHALL JUMP, TIM GOODYEAR,
and P. CRAIG RUSSELL

These stories take place during Buffy the Vampire Slayer's third and fourth seasons.

TITAN
BOOKS

"Food Chain" Part 1
writer christopher golden
penciller christian zanier
inker Andy owens
colorist guy major
letterer janice chiang

"The Latest Craze"
writers christopher golden
& Tom sniegoski
penciller cliff Richards
inker Joe pimentel
colorist guy major
letterer clem Robins

"Bad Dog"
writer Doug petrie
penciller Ryan sook
inker Tim goodyear
colorist guy major
letterer pat Brosseau

"The Food Chain" Part 2
writer christopher golden
penciller christian zanier
pencil assists marvin mariano
& Draxhall jump
inkers curtis p. Arnold, jason minor,
& Andy owens
colorist guy major
letterer Amador cisneros

"Double Cross"
writer Doug petrie
penciller jason minor
inker curtis p. Arnold
colorist guy major
letterer john costanza

"Punish Me with Kisses"
writers jamie s. Rich
& chynna clugston-major
artist chynna clugston-major
colorist guy major
letterer vickie williams

"One Small Promise"
writers Tom fassbender & jim pascoe
penciller cliff Richards
inker p. craig Russell
colorist guy major
letterer clem Robins

"City of Despair"
writers Tom fassbender & jim pascoe
penciller cliff Richards
inker Andy owens
colorist Lee Loughridge
letterer clem Robins

publisher Mike Richardson + *editor* scott Allie *with* Adam gallardo, Ben Abernathy, & Michael carriglitto + *art director* Mark cox + *designers* Keith wood & Amy Arendts

Special thanks to queen of worldwide publishing at 20th century-fox, Debbie olshan, David campiti, and caroline kallas and george snyder at *Buffy the vampire slayer*.

BUFFY THE VAMPIRE SLAYER: FOOD CHAIN
ISBN: 1 84023 315 X

published by Titan Books, a division of Titan publishing group Ltd.
144 southwark st
London SE1 0UP

A CIP catalogue record for this title is available from the British Library.

first edition september 2001
10 9 8 7 6 5 4 3 2 1

printed in Italy.

what did you think of this book? we love to hear from our readers.
please email us at: readerfeedback@titanemail.com or write to us at the above address.

Art by Randy Green *with* Tim Townsend *and* Guy Major

FOOD CHAIN PART I

EVIL'S A LOT LIKE ICE CREAM.
THE FISH TANK
YOU'VE GOT YOUR HUMAN EVIL, MORTAL PREDATORS, ALL OF THAT.
THEN YOU'VE GOT OTHER THINGS. THE THINGS EVEN THE PREDATORS FEAR. SHADOWS WITHIN SHADOWS, THINGS THAT GO BUMP IN THE NIGHT.
THEN YOU'VE GOT A MORE INSIDIOUS EVIL... THE SECRET. PEOPLE KNOWING HORRIBLE TRUTHS, AND NEVER SPEAKING THEM, DENYING THEM EVEN TO THEMSELVES.

EVIL'S A LOT LIKE ICE CREAM.
IT COMES IN SO MANY FLAVORS.
AND SUNNYDALE'S GOT EVERY ONE.
SUNNYDALE HOLDS ITS SECRETS CLOSE, PRAYING THE EVIL WILL GO AWAY. 'COURSE, THAT TRICK NEVER WORKS.
FORTUNATELY, SUNNYDALE HAS A LITTLE HELP WITH THE BIG EVILS. BUFFY SUMMERS. THE SLAYER. THE CHOSEN ONE.
DO IT, BRAD! DO IT!
OH YEAH, BRAD. BY ALL MEANS, DO IT.
YEAH, BUFFY'S JUST HELL ON THE BIG HONKIN' EVILS.

THE LITTLE ONES, THOUGH...
OH, NO, BUFFY...
THAT'S BRAD CAULFIELD'S CAR! COME BACK HERE, YOU JERK...
WHO'S GOING TO PAY FOR THIS?
YOU GOTTA BE KIDDING. CALLING MY MOM RICH IS SORT OF LIKE CALLING PRINCIPAL SNYDER TALL.
THAT'S NOT THE POINT, BUFFY. YOU AND YOUR MOM LIVE IN A NICE HOUSE IN A NICE NEIGHBORHOOD, AND SHE HAS HER OWN BUSINESS. TO A LOT OF KIDS WE KNOW, THAT *IS* RICH.
BRAD CAN BE PRETTY STUPID SOMETIMES, OKAY, A LOT OF THE TIME. BUT HE'S HAD IT PRETTY ROUGH. I'M NOT SAYING THAT MAKES IT OKAY. BUT... LOOK, I CAN GET HIM TO PAY YOUR MOM BACK IF...
KNOW WHAT? FORGET IT. I WAS FURIOUS, I'M OVER IT. BRAD WANTS TO BE A JERK TO IMPRESS HIS FRIENDS, *FINE*. I DON'T HAVE THE ENERGY TO WASTE STAYING MAD.
SWORD of SANNO
COOL. AND, LISTEN? ABOUT ME BEING IN THE CAR...
"BELIEVE ME, I'VE BEEN ALONG FOR THE RIDE A FEW TIMES AND WISHED I WAS ANYWHERE ELSE. GOTTA SAY, THOUGH, NOT LOVING BRAD."
MYSTERIES OF ANCIENT EGYPT
"AND YOU'RE WONDERING WHY I HANG WITH HIM AND HIS CREW, HUH? I DON'T KNOW, I GUESS... THEY GET ME, Y'KNOW? WHEN I FIRST MOVED HERE, THEY JUST LET ME IN.

"BESIDES, BUFFY, YOU DON'T EXACTLY HANG OUT WITH THE 'COOL' CROWD, EITHER."
"TOUCHÉ. I GUESS BRAD AND COMPANY JUST SEEM A LITTLE ROUGH AROUND THE EDGES IS ALL."
"Y'KNOW, I'M GLAD WE GOT A CHANCE TO TALK TODAY. I MEAN, YOU SEE SOMEONE IN THE HALLS, BUT YOU YOU NEVER KNOW THEM, REALLY."
"NO KIDDING. TWO GIRLS WITH BUSY SOCIAL CALENDARS LIKE US? I NEVER THOUGHT ABOUT HOW MUCH WE HAVE IN COMMON. I'VE BEEN THE NEW KID. I'VE BEEN THE REBEL."
REBEL? *Hmm* I THINK I LIKE THE SOUND OF--
WHOA, CAMEL. HOLD UP. THIS PART OF THE MUSEUM, I'VE SEEN. PYRAMIDS, SPHINXES... MUMMIES. I'LL PASS. BAD MEMORIES.
DO YOU THINK MR. BAIRD WILL NOTICE?
NOT IF WE TELL HIM WE WERE OVERCOME BY THE GRANDEUR OF FEUDAL JAPAN... AND BRING HIM A MOCHACCINO FROM THE LOBBY'S COFFEE SHOP.
SO, TELL ME AGAIN WHY YOU'RE ON THIS TRIP WHEN YOU'RE NOT EVEN IN MY CLASS?
I GOT IN A LITTLE TROUBLE THE END OF LAST YEAR... NOTHING I COULDN'T HANDLE... AND MISSED THE FIRST FEW WEEKS OF CLASSES THIS YEAR, WHEN *MY* HISTORY CLASS TOOK THIS TRIP.
HEY, YOU *ARE* A REBEL.

"...AND IT GOT ME THINKING. I MEAN, WHAT'S THE REAL DIFFERENCE BETWEEN ME AND SANDY SHIPMAN?"
THAT'D BE US.
THE COMPANY YOU KEEP IS QUESTIONABLE, BUT SANDY HANGS OUT WITH SOME REAL LOWLIFES.
MOST LIKELY TO BE IMPRISONED.
SEE, THAT'S WHAT I MEAN. OKAY, BRAD AND COMPANY-- THUGS AND MORONS--A GIVEN. BUT I GOT TO SPEND SOME TIME WITH SANDY, AND SHE'S--
SMART.
COOL.
A SMOKIN' HOTTY.
WHAT? IT'S TRUE, AND IF I DIDN'T COMMENT UPON HER OBVIOUS... ATTRIBUTES... YOU GUYS WOULD THINK SOME DEMON HAD SWITCHED ME WITH MY EVIL TWIN.

SANDY'S REALLY NICE, BUFFY. NOTHING LIKE THOSE CAVEMEN SHE HANGS OUT WITH. BUT IT'S SORT OF WELL, CAVEGIRL BY ASSOCIATION, Y'KNOW?
I JUST...DOESN'T SHE SEE IT? OKAY, I'VE BEEN IN TROUBLE, A LOT, BUT WITH THE WHOLE STANDING-AGAINST-THE-DARKNESS THING, THERE ISN'T MUCH THAT I CAN DO ABOUT IT.
SANDY'S BEEN HANGING WITH THOSE GUYS EVER SINCE SHE MOVED HERE. I CAN'T CHANGE MY LIFE, BUT SHE COULD CHANGE HERS.
"SHE'S GOT SO MUCH GOING FOR HER, DOESN'T SHE SEE THAT THEY'RE DRAGGING HER DOWN?"
WHICH I GUESS MEANS THAT, WITH YOUR BAD-GIRL REP AND ALL, HANGING OUT WITH US IS KINDA LIKE DRAGGING YOU UP, HUH?
Xander...
AND THEY SAY I HAVE NO TACT.

BRRRINGG
Hey.
BUFFY, HI. WHAT'S UP?
JUST SAW YOU SITTING HERE WITHOUT THE BEASTIE BOYS FOR ONCE, FIGURED I'D SAY HEY. IT WAS COOL, HANGING OUT YESTERDAY. MAYBE WE CAN DO IT AGAIN SOME TIME?
YEAH. THAT'D BE--
SANDY LET'S GO.
I DON'T KNOW IF THE CANDLES ARE EXACTLY RIGHT, BUT...
SEE YOU LATER, THEN, SANDY I--
HEY, BRAD. NEXT TIME, I'D APPRECIATE IT IF YOU LEFT LANDSCAPING TO THE EXPERTS.
YEAH, WHATEVER. C'MON, SANDY. WE'VE GOT A LOT TO DO BEFORE TONIGHT.

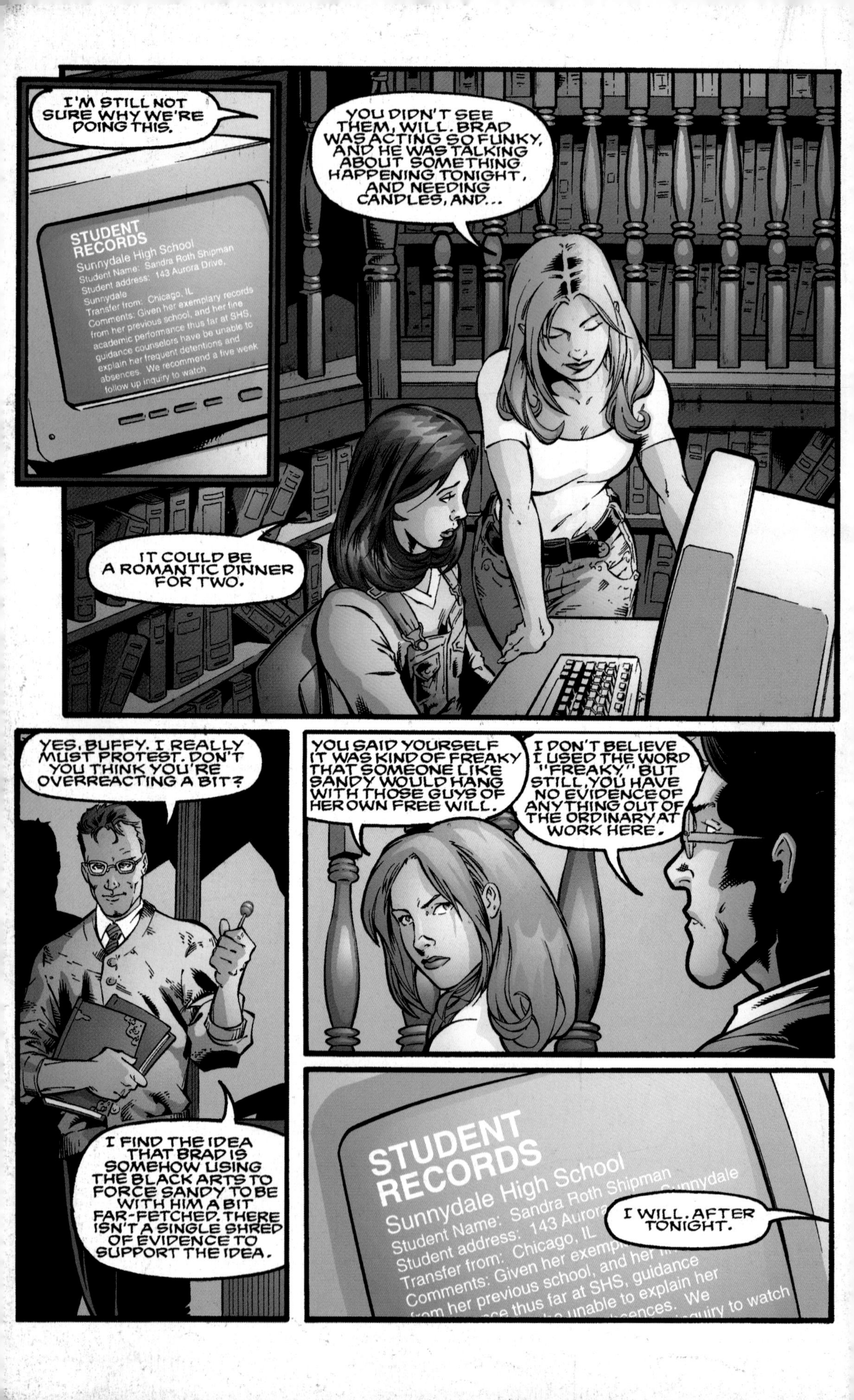
I'M STILL NOT SURE WHY WE'RE DOING THIS.
STUDENT RECORDS
Sunnydale High School
Student Name: Sandra Roth Shipman
Student address: 143 Aurora Drive, Sunnydale
Transfer from: Chicago, IL
Comments: Given her exemplary records from her previous school, and her fine academic performance thus far at SHS, guidance counselors have be unable to explain her frequent detentions and absences. We recommend a five week follow up inquiry to watch
YOU DIDN'T SEE THEM, WILL. BRAD WAS ACTING SO FUNKY, AND HE WAS TALKING ABOUT SOMETHING HAPPENING TONIGHT, AND NEEDING CANDLES, AND...
IT COULD BE A ROMANTIC DINNER FOR TWO.
YES, BUFFY. I REALLY MUST PROTEST. DON'T YOU THINK YOU'RE OVERREACTING A BIT?
I FIND THE IDEA THAT BRAD IS SOMEHOW USING THE BLACK ARTS TO FORCE SANDY TO BE WITH HIM A BIT FAR-FETCHED. THERE ISN'T A SINGLE SHRED OF EVIDENCE TO SUPPORT THE IDEA.
YOU SAID YOURSELF IT WAS KIND OF FREAKY THAT SOMEONE LIKE SANDY WOULD HANG WITH THOSE GUYS OF HER OWN FREE WILL.
I DON'T BELIEVE I USED THE WORD "FREAKY," BUT STILL, YOU HAVE NO EVIDENCE OF ANYTHING OUT OF THE ORDINARY AT WORK HERE.
STUDENT RECORDS
Sunnydale High School
Student Name: Sandra Roth Shipman
I WILL. AFTER TONIGHT.

MARDUK, LORD OF VICTORY OVER THE DARK ANGELS, REMEMBER!
MARDUK, SON OF ENKI, MASTER OF MAGICIANS, REMEMBER!
MARDUK, VANQUISHER OF THE ANCIENT ONES, REMEMBER!
MARDUK, WHO ASSIGNS THE WANDERERS THEIR PLACES, REMEMBER!
IN THE NAME OF THE COVENANT SWORN BETWEEN THEE AND THE RACE OF MEN...

WE CALL TO THEE, HARKEN AND REMEMBER.
WE CALL TO THEE, HARKEN AND REMEMBER.

WHO DARES...?
KRAK
HOPE YOU DON'T MIND. I LET MYSELF IN.
HOME SWEET HOME

Y'KNOW, MOST OF THE MORONS WHO DABBLE IN DARK MAGIC AT LEAST GET POINTS FOR IMAGINATION. YOU GUYS EVER THINK, OKAY, ARCANE POWER...
MAYBE YOU COULD *EACH* GET A GIRL?
BUFFY, *NO!* DON'T TOUCH!
FZZZT!
YOU STUPID COW!

LOOK WHAT YOU'VE DONE.
YOU'VE RUINED THEM. RUINED IT ALL.
YEAH.
KRASSH
I GUESS I'M JUST CLUMSY THAT WAY.

BRAD, SORRY ABOUT THE MISUNDERSTANDING. I PROMISE TO MAKE IT UP TO YOU IF YOU LIVE THROUGH THIS... YOU CAN WAKE UP NOW.
GUYS?
YOU JUST SIT TIGHT WHILE I CALL OUT THE UPTIGHT BRITISH CAVALRY, OKAY?
OH, OF COURSE.
THE ONE TIME I LISTEN TO GILES' ADVICE NOT TO "SLAY FIRST, ASK QUESTIONS LATER..." THAT OUGHTA TEACH ME.

...SLAYER IS A PRETTY SIMPLE JOB DESCRIPTION, GILES. IF I'D KEPT THAT IN MIND, I COULD BE HOME WORKING ON MY AMERICAN HEROES TERM PAPER RIGHT NOW.
"WE ALL MAKE MISTAKES."? THAT'S THE BEST YOU CAN DO? YOU NEVER DID GET THE WHOLE PEP-TALK/ MORALE BOOSTER THING DOWN, DID YOU?
SO DO YOU THINK WILLOW CAN HELP?
GOOD. SEE YOU SOON.
UNLESS, OF COURSE, SOMETHING VERY BAD HAPPENS TO ME, IN WHICH CASE, I WON'T.
IT'S THAT KIND OF NIGHT.

THANKS FOR GETTING HERE SO FAST. GILES IS DOING THE RESEARCH?
NOW THAT WE KNOW SANDY'S THE EVIL ONE AND NOT BRAD, HE SAID HE HAD SOME IDEAS.
THAT'S A START.
WILLOW, SEE IF THERE ARE ANY SPELLS OR WHATEVER YOU CAN USE TO WAKE THESE GUYS UP. OZ, XANDER, YOU GUYS ARE HERE TO MAKE SURE NOTHING HAPPENS TO WILLOW. JUST IN CASE.
YOUR WISH IS MY COMMAND, O CHOSEN ONE. ESPECIALLY IF IT'S SOMETHING NAUGHTY.
WHERE ARE YOU GOING TO BE?
HUNTING.

WOW. JUST MAKE YOURSELF AT HOME, WILL. FIND EVERYTHING YOU NEEDED?
PRETTY MUCH. OUR GIRL SANDY ISN'T JUST A DEMON. SHE'S A THINK-AHEAD KIND OF DEMON. SHE KEPT THE CUPBOARD PRETTY WELL-STOCKED WITH THE MAGICAL BASICS.
I'M THINKING YOU SHOULD HURRY. HARD TO TELL, BUT I'D SAY CONNOR'S DEAD AND THE OTHER GUYS MIGHT NOT BE FAR BEHIND.
OH...
...NO...

NOW, WHERE DID I PUT THE CODEX?
AH, YES. WILLOW HAD IT LAST.
HERE WE ARE. NOW LET'S--
WAIT A MOMENT. "SANDRA ROTH SHIPMAN." SANDRA ROTH. WHY DOES THAT SOUND SO...
OH, NO.
SANDRA ROTH
BEEPBEEPBEEPBE

"GILES, IT'S ME, WHAT'S--"
"BUFFY, LISTEN CAREFULLY. THE DEMON'S NAME IS YLISANDROTH. IT'S ONE OF THE LOWER CREATURES. IN ORDER TO SURVIVE ON THIS PLANE, IT MUST GET ITS ENERGIES FROM OTHERS.
"IT USES THE BLACK ARTS TO SURROUND ITSELF WITH ADMIRERS, AND FEEDS OFF OF THEM."
"SOUNDS A LOT LIKE CORDELIA, ACTUALLY. WE SHOULD LOOK INTO--"
"YOU'RE NOT PAYING ATTENTION, BUFFY. IT CAN'T SURVIVE ON THIS PLANE WITHOUT THOSE ENERGIES. YOU INTERRUPTED THE RITUAL. THERE ISN'T TIME FOR IT TO START AGAIN.
"IT'S GOING TO HAVE TO GO BACK FOR BRAD AND THE OTHERS, WHICH MEANS... BUFFY... ARE YOU THERE? BUFFY..."

YLISANDROTH. LET THEM GO.
AH, BUFFY, GLAD YOU COULD MAKE IT. YOU SAID YOU WANTED TO HANG OUT AGAIN. HERE'S OUR CHANCE.
PLEASE HAVE A SEAT. WE'RE AT A CRUCIAL STAGE IN THE RITUAL. OH, AND YOU SHOULD KNOW THAT IF YOU INTERFERE NOW, WHAT HAPPENED BEFORE WILL SEEM TAME.
PLEASE HAVE A SEAT. YOU'LL BREAK THE CIRCUIT, AND YOUR FRIENDS WILL DIE. IF YOU TRY TO REMOVE YOUR FRIENDS FROM THE CIRCLE, THEY'LL DIE.

THANKS FOR THE ADVICE.
SHHLIKKT!

HEY, YOU SCRUBS, WAIT UP!
NO WAY, DUDE!
BUFFY, THAT'S JUST...DISGUSTING. AND, OKAY, AMAZING, BUT PLEASE TELL ME YOUR AIM HAD MORE TO DO WITH SLAYER SKILL THAN LUCK.
SO, I GUESS CONNOR WASN'T DEAD AFTER ALL.
OR ISN'T ANYMORE. YOU NEVER KNOW WITH THIS SORT OF THING.
WELL, I GUESS THAT'S THE LAST TIME I'LL STICK MY NOSE INTO SOMEONE ELSE'S BUSINESS.
OR NOT.
SO...
WHO WANTS ICE CREAM?

Art by Cliff Richards *with* Joe Fabio Laguna *and* Guy Major

THE LASTEST CRAZE

SUNNYDALE, CALIFORNIA. IT'S A NICE PLACE TO VISIT.
BUT NOT AFTER DARK.
ALL KINDS OF THINGS GO ON AROUND HERE WHEN THE SUN GOES DOWN.
THE PEOPLE OF SUNNYDALE TURN A BLIND EYE, AND WAIT FOR DAWN.
SO IT'S NO SURPRISE, REALLY, THAT NOBODY PAYS ANY ATTENTION TO THE ARRIVAL OF A SINGLE, UNREMARK-ABLE VEHICLE.
BUT THEY'RE GOING TO WISH THEY HAD.
I'M TELLIN' YOU, LADS... YOU'RE GONNA BE BIG.

SLAYER!!!
WHERE IS SHE? I WILL SPARE THE LIFE OF THE FIRST TO SPEAK. TELL ME WHERE THE SLAYER HAS GONE.
SPIRITS OF THE STORM, PROTECT YOUR SUPPLICANTS! WE BOW BEFORE THEE, CRADLED IN THE SILENCE OF YOUR EYE!
THAT OUGHTTA DO IT.
YOU KNOW, YOU'RE KINDA CUTE WHEN YOU'RE SPELLCASTING.
HAVE YOU CHECKED THE CUSHIONS ON THE SOFA? I'M ALWAYS LOSING STUFF DOWN THERE.
XANDER, NOW'S NOT THE TIME. AND HE DOES HAVE A POINT. IT WOULD BE HELPFUL TO KNOW JUST WHERE BUFFY HAS GOTTEN OFF TO.
W
S
N
E
BUFFY SUMMERS KIND OF LIKES THE RAIN. WHEN YOU LIVE IN SOUTHERN CALIFORNIA, IT'S SORT OF A NOVELTY. STORY OF HER LIFE...
SNAP
ANYTHING SHE LIKES, EVEN THE SMALLEST THING, EVENTUALLY SOME DEMON HAS TO COME ALONG AND SCREW IT UP.
WHERE IS THE SLAYER?!

THAT'S ME. MISS POPULARITY.
YOU THINK IT'S EASY CLIMBING UP ON A ROOF. IN THE WIND. AND THE RAIN. IN *THESE* SHOES?
GHAHHH!
OOOF.
WHUD
Y'KNOW, THERE ARE A LOT OF DRAWBACKS TO BEING THE CHOSEN ONE, BUT ONE OF THE WORST IS IT'S HELL ON MY WARDROBE.
HOW SAD. YOU MUST HAVE SPENT HOURS RUMMAGING THROUGH THE GOODWILL BINS TO FIND THOSE PANTS. CAN WE GO NOW?

SO I'M THINKIN' POSSIBLY BRONZE TONIGHT.
THAT'D BE GREAT. YOU'VE BEEN M.I.A. SINCE THE WHOLE DJINN THING LAST WEEK.
GILES HAD ME PATROLLING MY BRAINS OUT, IN CASE IT CAME BACK. BUT NO SIGN OF THE UGLY WEATHERMAN, SO, HOPEFULLY, BRONZE.
I WANTED TO LOOK MY CALC NOTES OVER ONE MORE TIME BEFORE THE TEST. YOU HEADED TO THE LIBRARY?
YEP. GILES AND I ARE GOING TO HAVE A LITTLE MEETING OF THE MINDS THAT WILL END WITH ME AT THE BRONZE TONIGHT, COME HELL OR HIGH WATER.
WHICH, AROUND HERE, YA NEVER KNOW.
...JUST CAN'T GET OVER HOW CUTE HE IS, ELISSA.
HE OUGHTTA BE CUTE FOR WHAT HE COST, THOUGH. I MEAN, YOU HANG HIM FROM YOUR BAG, AND THAT'S THAT.
LISTEN TO YOU! HOW MANY OF THOSE STUPID BEANIES ARE COLLECTING DUST ON THE BOOK-SHELF IN YOUR BEDROOM?
BESIDES, IT'S GOOD THAT HOOLIGANS ARE EXPENSIVE. THAT MEANS ONLY PEOPLE WITH ENOUGH MONEY TO APPRECIATE THEM CAN AFFORD ONE. RIGHT, JEREMY?
YOU WERE THE BEST HOOLIGAN IN THE STORE. WE'RE THE PERFECT TEAM. WE BOTH INSPIRE ENVY.
SO WHAT YOU'RE SAYING IS HOOLIGANS AREN'T TOYS, THEY'RE STATUS SYMBOLS?
HELLO? WELCOME TO THIS CONVERSATION.
WELL WHY DIDN'T YOU JUST SAY SO? SOMETIMES YOU'RE SO OBTUSE. SO, WAIT, DID YOU SAY THEY HAD LIMITED EDITIONS COMING IN?
"NOT FOR ANOTHER WEEK OR SO."
"COOL. WHERE'S THE STORE AGAIN?"

OKAY, THE TOY WAS NOT LOOKING AT ME.
HE WAS KIND OF CUTE, THOUGH.
HOOLIGAN HOVEL
The Authorized Carrier of All Things Hooligan
"THIS ISN'T LIKE YOU, WILLOW. YOU'RE A BRIGHT GIRL. WHY WOULD YOU SPEND ALL THAT MONEY ON SOMETHING SO RIDICULOUSLY IMPRACTICAL?"
OH, SO I'M RIDICULOUS NOW? THANKS SO MUCH. WELL YOU KNOW WHAT? IT'S MY MONEY, MOM, AND I'LL SPEND IT IF I WANT TO!
FINE. BUT YOU'RE GOING TO FEEL AWFULLY SILLY WHEN THIS LITTLE FAD IS OVER.
IT'S NOT A FAD!
SLAM
WOW. OKAY, TEENAGE DAUGHTER EQUALS REBELLION, BUT...
WOW. WHERE DID THAT COME FROM?
YOU'RE THE ONLY ONE WHO UNDERSTANDS ME, ALEISTER.

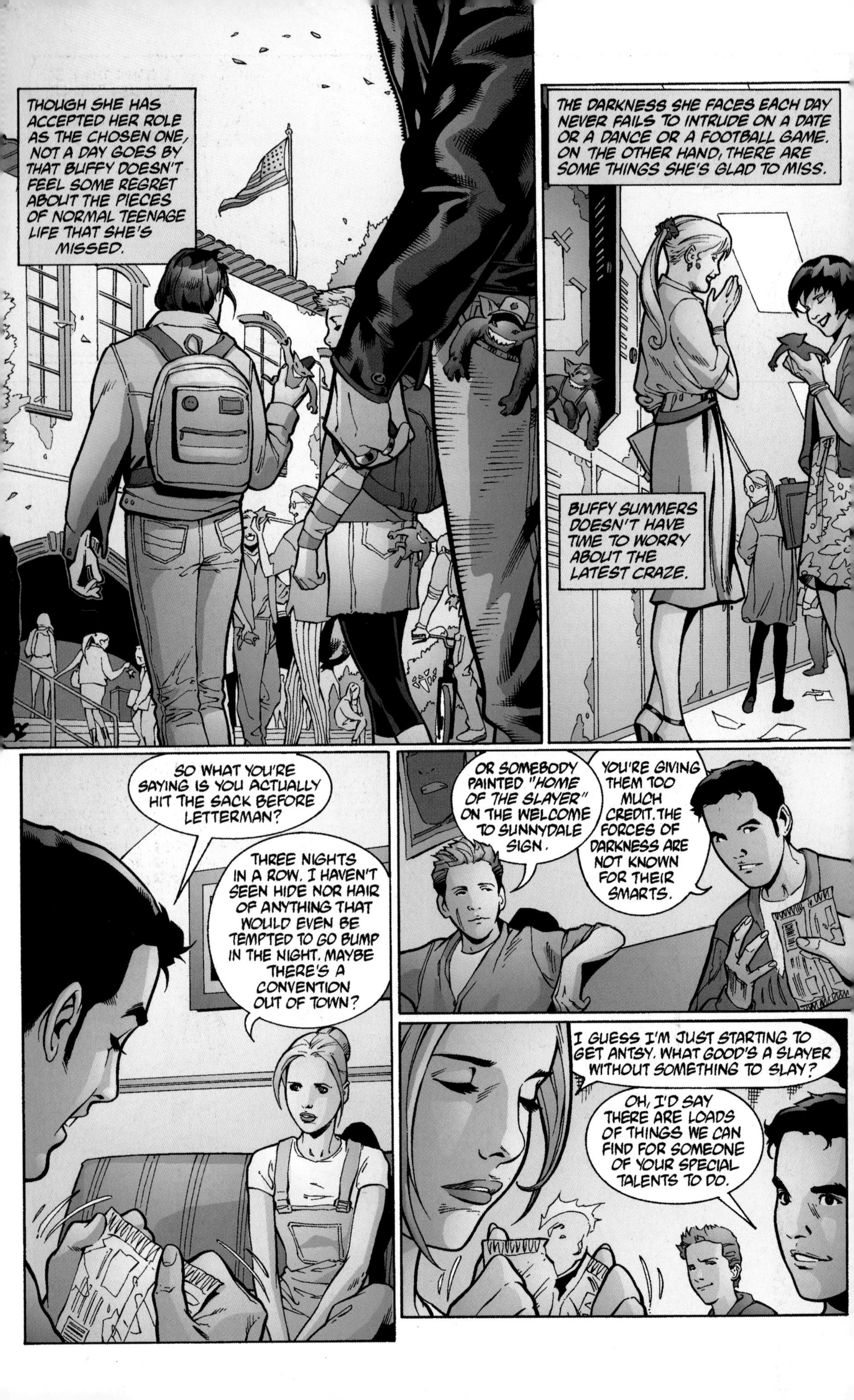

THOUGH SHE HAS ACCEPTED HER ROLE AS THE CHOSEN ONE, NOT A DAY GOES BY THAT BUFFY DOESN'T FEEL SOME REGRET ABOUT THE PIECES OF NORMAL TEENAGE LIFE THAT SHE'S MISSED.
THE DARKNESS SHE FACES EACH DAY NEVER FAILS TO INTRUDE ON A DATE OR A DANCE OR A FOOTBALL GAME. ON THE OTHER HAND, THERE ARE SOME THINGS SHE'S GLAD TO MISS.
BUFFY SUMMERS DOESN'T HAVE TIME TO WORRY ABOUT THE LATEST CRAZE.
SO WHAT YOU'RE SAYING IS YOU ACTUALLY HIT THE SACK BEFORE LETTERMAN?
THREE NIGHTS IN A ROW. I HAVEN'T SEEN HIDE NOR HAIR OF ANYTHING THAT WOULD EVEN BE TEMPTED TO GO BUMP IN THE NIGHT. MAYBE THERE'S A CONVENTION OUT OF TOWN?
OR SOMEBODY PAINTED "HOME OF THE SLAYER" ON THE WELCOME TO SUNNYDALE SIGN.
YOU'RE GIVING THEM TOO MUCH CREDIT. THE FORCES OF DARKNESS ARE NOT KNOWN FOR THEIR SMARTS.
I GUESS I'M JUST STARTING TO GET ANTSY. WHAT GOOD'S A SLAYER WITHOUT SOMETHING TO SLAY?
OH, I'D SAY THERE ARE LOADS OF THINGS WE CAN FIND FOR SOMEONE OF YOUR SPECIAL TALENTS TO DO.

HEY GUYS. EVERYONE READY FOR THE HISTORY TEST? I'M KINDA STOKED.
I DON'T THINK I'D EVER USE "STOKED" AND "TEST" IN THE SAME SENTENCE, BUT I THINK I'M SET. WHO'S YOUR LITTLE FRIEND?
THIS IS ALEISTER! HE'S MY--
--HOOLIGAN. OH, PLEASE, WILLOW. COME ON. BETTER TO BE HOOLIGAN-LESS THAN TO BUY THE BOTTOM OF THE LINE.
WHAT'S THE MATTER, CORDY? GETTING ALL I'LL-GET-YOU-MY-PRETTY JUST 'CAUSE YOU WERE SNOOZIN' WHEN THE FAD TRAIN PULLED INTO TOWN?
HE'S CUTE. IN AN UGLY KIND OF WAY. I HOPE THAT'S NOT MY COMPETITION.
I'LL TELL YOU WHAT'S UGLY. ALL THE LITTLE ACCESSORIES THEY HAVE FOR THESE THINGS AT HOOLIGAN HOVEL. THEY'LL JUST MILK EVERY DOLLAR OUT OF IT UNTIL IT DIES.
AND ANYWAY, IT'S ONLY WORTH HAVING ONE IF YOU HAVE THE MOST EXPENSIVE ONE, A TITANIUM LIMITED EDITION. WHICH, OF COURSE, I HAVE ON ORDER AS WE SPEAK.
OF COURSE YOU--

DON'T YOU TOUCH ALEISTER! HE'S MINE!
OH PLEASE. HE'S NOTHING SPECIAL, WILLOW. STANDARD ISSUE.
WHOA, WILL. DOWN, GIRL. IT'S JUST A DOLL.
IT'S NOT JUST A DOLL.
SORRY. I GUESS I MUST BE NERVOUS ABOUT THE TEST AFTER ALL.
YOU LITTLE SKANK! I CAN'T BELIEVE YOU DID IT!
SO MUCH FOR QUIET.
GET AWAY FROM ME, YOU STUPID APE. I BOUGHT IT, FAIR AND SQUARE.
I'VE HAD MY EYE ON THAT ONE FOR WEEKS! I'VE BEEN SAVING UP! JUST BECAUSE YOUR PARENTS ARE FILTHY RICH, YOU THINK YOU CAN JUST HAVE ANYTHING YOU WANT.
AND YOUR POINT WOULD BE?
HEY, SPORT. YOU WANNA PICK ON GIRLS HALF YOUR SIZE, TRY ME.
LEMME GO, YOU CRAZY WITCH!
WHAT'S ALL THIS ABOUT?

YOU SNOOZE, YOU LOSE, MORON. THEY ONLY HAD ONE HOOLIGAN LIKE THIS, AND I WAS GONNA HAVE IT. IT WAS WORTH THE THREE HUNDRED DOLLARS JUST TO SEE HOW JEALOUS EVERYONE IS.
YOU DON'T GET IT! I WAS SAVING UP. THAT'S A PLATINUM LIMITED EDITION.
THREE HUNDRED DOLLARS? EVERY-THING I OWN DOESN'T ADD UP TO THREE HUNDRED DOLLARS.
AND YOU WERE GONNA SPEND THAT ON A DOLL?
NOT THAT THERE'S ANYTHING WRONG WITH THAT.
MAYBE THEY STILL HAVE ONE OF THE FOOTBALL HOOLIGANS, YEAH. THAT'D BE COOL.
PLATINUM, HUH? I HAVE ONE OF THE TITANIUM EDITIONS ON ORDER.
AM I THE ONLY ONE WHO THOUGHT THAT WAS A BIT STRANGE?
IF YOUR DEFINITION OF "A BIT STRANGE" INCLUDES HAVING EVERY-THING YOU THOUGHT YOU UNDERSTOOD THRASHED WITHIN AN INCH OF ITS LIFE ...THEN NO, YOU'RE NOT THE ONLY ONE.

BONG BONG BONG BONG
BONG BONG BONG
COMICS
BONG BONG BONG
BONG BONG
BONG
SHOES
Something
RFA 59
BOB

I'M SORRY, GUYS... CRYING IS SO EMBARRASSING, AND MESSY. BUT MY GRANDMOTHER GAVE ME THAT BRACELET. IT'S THE ONLY THING I HAVE OF HERS, AND NOW IT'S JUST GONE...
YOU'LL FIND IT, ELISSA. AND, LOOK ON THE BRIGHT SIDE. AT LEAST YOU'VE STILL GOT JEREMY TO CHEER YOU UP.
YEAH. GUESS YOU'RE RIGHT. ≷SNIFF≶ I DON'T KNOW WHAT I'D DO WITHOUT HIM. OKAY, CORDELIA'S NEW ONE MAY BE MORE EXPENSIVE -- THE WITCH -- BUT JEREMY JUST MAKES EVERYTHING OKAY.
HE'S THE ONLY ONE WHO UNDERSTANDS. IT'S LIKE MAGIC...
WHAT'S THE MATTER WITH YOU? I ASKED FOR A CHILI DOG. I DIDN'T ASK YOU TO SPLATTER CHILI ON THELONIUS! THE SCHOOL IS GOING TO PAY TO REPLACE HIM!
ALL I WANTED WAS A CHILI DOG...
SOMEONE WOKE UP CRANKY.
APPARENTLY, SOMEONE IS SUFFERING FROM CAFETERIA AMNESIA. ASKING FOR THIS STUFF IS A LITTLE LIKE ELECTIVE SURGERY.
HI, GUYS.
HEY, I'M WITNESSING SAD FACE. WHAT'S UP?

I ALMOST DON'T WANT TO TELL YOU, BUT... PEZ-WITCH IS GONE.
I'M SURE IT'LL TURN UP, WILL. SHE DIDN'T JUST UP AND FLY AWAY. NOT UNLESS SHE COMES WITH A PEZ BROOM-STICK.
IT'S OKAY.
I KNOW. OKAY, CANDY AND PLASTIC. BUT IT WAS THE FIRST THING YOU EVER GAVE ME AND, WELL, SENTIMENTAL VALUE AND ALL.
IF IT IS LOST, WE CAN ALWAYS GET YOU ANOTHER ONE.
FESTIVAL
OR, Y'KNOW, SOMETHING ELSE EQUALLY COOL. LIKE MAY-BE A COMPLETE SET OF HOLO-GRAPHIC, CHROME HOOLIGAN TRADING CARDS.
ALSO NICE. THEN AGAIN THERE'S THAT APPOINT-MENT WITH THE PSYCHIATRIST YOU SO DESPERATELY NEED.

HEE HEE HEH
SSSHHHH.
OOOOOOH.
UHNGGHHH.
AAAAAAH.

UNNHH...
YAH YAH.
YAH YAH.
WHAT THE HECK?
THAT WAS A PRETTY VIVID DREAM...
...MY RING!
NOT MY RING!

MAYBE IT WASN'T A DREAM AFTER...
NOW THIS IS CREEPY. WHERE DID YOU COME FROM?
I KNOW YOU DIDN'T WALK IN.
I WONDER IF THIS IS SOMEBODY'S FREAKY IDEA OF AN EVEN TRADE?
AS IF.
I DON'T CARE HOW MUCH YOU COST.
THAT RING'S PRICELESS TO ME.
HOOLIGAN HOVEL
The A rized Carrier of All Things Hooligan
MOM, LOOK, I GOT MINE THE SPACE SUIT!
I GOT MINE THE LAVENDER HOOLIGAN SPICE HOT PANTS.

HOT PANTS.
THIS MUST BE THE PLACE.
HI! WELCOME TO HOOLIGAN HOVEL, THE AUTHORIZED CARRIER OF ALL THINGS HOOLIGAN. ARE YOU LOOKING FOR SOMETHING SPECIAL FOR YOUR LITTLE FRIEND?
UHH. YEAH.
YOU'RE IN LUCK! WE JUST GOT A SHIPMENT OF NEW MERCHANDICE, INCLUDING HOOLIGAN BUBBLE BATH, THE HOOLIGAN DENTISTRY KIT-- TO KEEP THOSE CHOPPERS SHINY, AND THE HOOLIGAN BEACH HOVEL WITH REAL WORKING JACUZZI. IT'S AWESOME.
EVERYBODY WHO'S ANYONE IS BUYING IT. AND IF YOU'RE LOOKING FOR THE LATEST IN HOOLIGAN FASHIONS--
I'D HAVE TO BE RICH. DO PEOPLE REALLY PAY THESE PRICES FOR ALL THIS STUFF WITHOUT YOU HOLDING A GUN TO THEIR HEADS?
OH, YOU'D BE SURPRISED. HOOLIGANS JUST MAKE PEOPLE HAPPY. AND MOST OF THESE ITEMS ARE LIMITED EDITION COLLECTIBLES, NOT AVAILABLE AT ANY OTHER STORE. IT'S AWESOME.
YEAH. AWESOME.
APPARENTLY, I'M THE ONLY ONE IN TOWN WHO THINKS YOU'RE AN UGLY, CREEPY LITTLE THING.

OKAY, HAVE AN AWESOME DAY! THANKS FOR STOPPING BY HOOLIGAN HOVEL, THE AUTHORIZED CARRIER OF ALL THINGS HOOLIGAN!
YOU CAN COME OUT NOW, BOSS. SHE'S GONE. I DIDN'T THINK SHE WAS MEAN, THOUGH. I THOUGHT SHE WAS KIND OF NICE. SHE HAD A CUTE HOOLIGAN...
WOULD YOU CEASE YOUR INANE PRATTLING, AND GET BACK TO STOCKING THE SHELVES?!
SURE THING, MR. RAYNE, RIGHT AWAY.
DON'T TOUCH MY HOOLIGAN, YOU FREAK! YOU WANT ONE, BUY ONE!
HOOLIGAN NIGHT
BRING YOUR HOOLIGAN
DRINKS 1/2 PRICE
WOULD YOU BELIEVE AURA DOESN'T EVEN HAVE A HOOLIGAN?
SHE'S A CULTURAL CRIPPLE. SHE'S STILL TRYING TO KEEP THAT KEYCHAIN THING ALIVE.
DOES ANYONE ELSE FEEL LIKE WE'RE AT ZOMBIE FAIR '99? I DON'T KNOW, MAYBE I'M HALLUCINATING, BUT EVERYONE'S ACTING KINDA FUNKY.
YEAH, LAST I CHECKED, BRINGING YOUR TOYS TO THE LOCAL HOT SPOT WASN'T PART OF THE REPERTOIRE OF COOL.

SEE, NOW YOU'RE SCARING ME, 'CAUSE THAT'S JUST WHAT I WAS THINKING. COLOR ME CRAZY, BUT SEEMS TO ME ONLY THE POPULAR KIDS ARE ACTING WEIRD. POPULAR MEANING RICH.
RICH MEANING, "NOW OWNS A HOOLIGAN." I'M WILLING TO BET ALL THE WACKINESS HAS SOMETHING TO DO WITH THE UGLY LITTLE THINGS.
HOW CAN YOU EVEN SAY THAT? THAT'S SO... NOT NICE!
WILLOW'S NOT POPULAR OR RICH, SO THERE! YOU'RE JUST JEALOUS 'CAUSE YOU CAN'T AFFORD ONE.
YEAH, COR, THAT'S EXACTLY IT. ON THE NOSE. ACTUALLY, THOUGH, I DO HAVE ONE. DON'T KNOW WHERE I GOT IT, BUT--
SO YOU HAVE ONE, AND YOU'RE NOT ACTING AS PETTY AND COMPULSIVE AND... OKAY, I'LL SAY IT, OBSESSED... AS CERTAIN OTHER PEOPLE WE KNOW.
I MEAN, SOMEONE STEALS PEZ-WITCH AND CHROMIUM HOOLIGAN CARDS ARE A SUITABLE REPLACEMENT? WHAT'S UP WITH THAT?
WHAT, NOW YOU'RE JUDGING WHETHER OR NOT I GRIEVED ENOUGH FOR PEZ-WITCH? YOU THINK ALEISTER HAS SOME KIND OF MAGICAL HOLD ON ME OR SOMETHING?
PRETTY MUCH. YEP.
THAT'S RIDICULOUS! BUFFY HAS A HOOLIGAN, AND SHE'S BEEN WHINING ABOUT LOSING THAT CHEAP LITTLE RING ANGEL GAVE HER EVER SINCE WE GOT IN HERE.
I WAS GONNA SAY THAT.
TRUE, BUT BUFFY'S ALSO THE SLAYER. IF THESE THINGS ARE MAKING EVERYONE ACT FREAKY, MAYBE THEY CAN'T AFFECT HER.

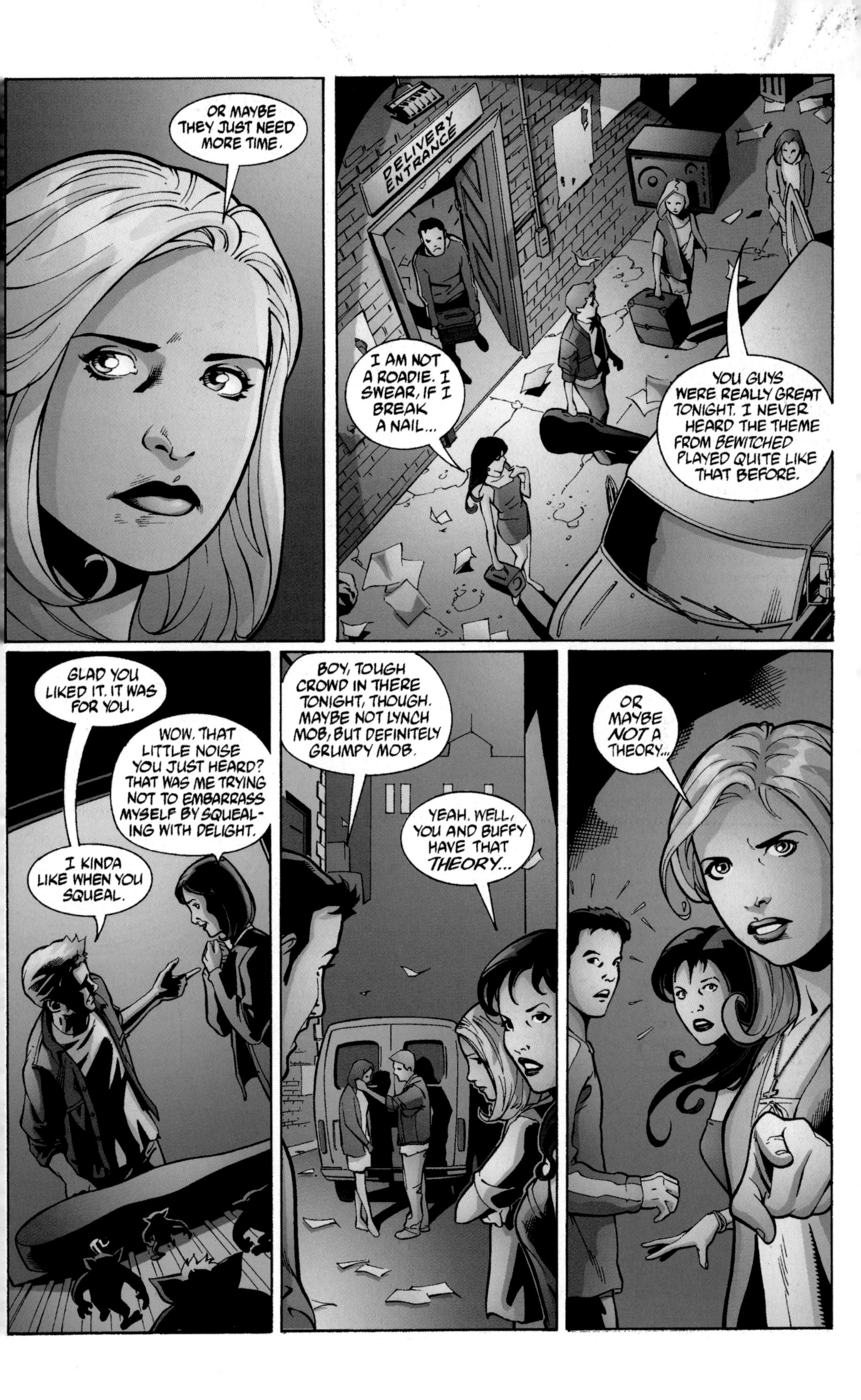
OR MAYBE THEY JUST NEED MORE TIME.
DELIVERY ENTRANCE
I AM NOT A ROADIE. I SWEAR, IF I BREAK A NAIL...
YOU GUYS WERE REALLY GREAT TONIGHT. I NEVER HEARD THE THEME FROM *BEWITCHED* PLAYED QUITE LIKE THAT BEFORE.
GLAD YOU LIKED IT. IT WAS FOR YOU.
WOW. THAT LITTLE NOISE YOU JUST HEARD? THAT WAS ME TRYING NOT TO EMBARRASS MYSELF BY SQUEALING WITH DELIGHT.
I KINDA LIKE WHEN YOU SQUEAL.
BOY, TOUGH CROWD IN THERE TONIGHT, THOUGH. MAYBE NOT LYNCH MOB, BUT DEFINITELY GRUMPY MOB.
YEAH. WELL, YOU AND BUFFY HAVE THAT *THEORY*...
OR MAYBE *NOT* A THEORY...

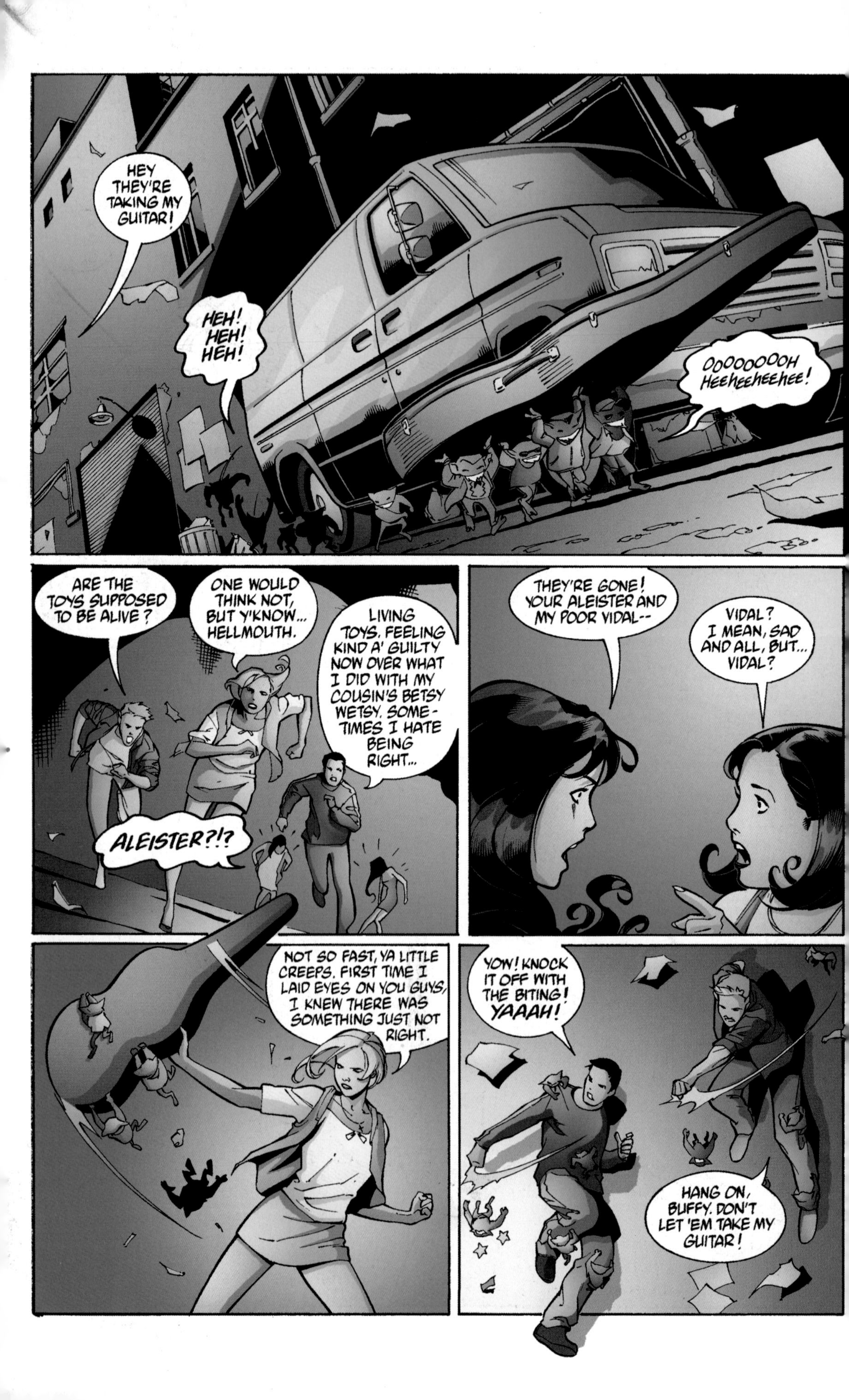
HEY THEY'RE TAKING MY GUITAR!
HEH! HEH! HEH!
OOOOOOOOH Heeheeheehee!
ARE THE TOYS SUPPOSED TO BE ALIVE?
ONE WOULD THINK NOT, BUT Y'KNOW... HELLMOUTH.
LIVING TOYS. FEELING KIND A' GUILTY NOW OVER WHAT I DID WITH MY COUSIN'S BETSY WETSY. SOMETIMES I HATE BEING RIGHT...
ALEISTER?!?
THEY'RE GONE! YOUR ALEISTER AND MY POOR VIDAL--
VIDAL? I MEAN, SAD AND ALL, BUT... VIDAL?
NOT SO FAST, YA LITTLE CREEPS. FIRST TIME I LAID EYES ON YOU GUYS, I KNEW THERE WAS SOMETHING JUST NOT RIGHT.
YOW! KNOCK IT OFF WITH THE BITING! YAAAH!
HANG ON, BUFFY. DON'T LET 'EM TAKE MY GUITAR!

DOING MY BEST... BUT THESE LITTLE GUYS HAVE NO RESPECT FOR AUTHORITY... AND NAUGHTY HANDS...
NOW LEGGO, YOU--
PTOOIE!
EEEEEW!
HEE HEE HEE, HEH HA HA HA!
GET BACK HERE!
UM, OZ... STILL HAVING A PROBLEM HERE... HELP!

CRAP...
...THEY'RE FAST.
AND ALSO ...GROSS.
I JUST CAN'T BELIEVE IT. XANDER AND BUFFY WERE RIGHT!
I KNOW. IT'S JUST...VIDAL WOULD NEVER DO ANY-THING BAD.
YUP. THOSE POOR LITTLE GUYS MUST'VE JUST FALLEN IN WITH THE WRONG CROWD.
I'M THINKING EXTERMINATOR.
OR THE NEXT BEST THING.
NOK NOK
HOLD ON, HOLD ON. DON'T GET YOUR KNICKERS IN A TWIST.

BUFFY? DO YOU HAVE ANY IDEA WHAT--
TOY? I DON'T THINK SO.
ANY IDEA WHAT THIS THING IS?
...I CONFESS I NEVER DREAMED I'D SEE ONE OF THESE. THE JAPANESE CALLED THEM BAKEMONO, BUT MOST OF THE LEGENDS COME FROM GERMANY, WHERE THEY WERE CALLED BAUMESEL.
NASTY LITTLE GITS. DIDN'T THINK THERE WERE ANY LEFT IN THIS DIMENSION. THEY'RE REPUTED TO MAKE THEIR HOMES IN THE HOLLOWS OF TREES. WITH THEIR MOTHER, OF COURSE.
THEIR MOTHER?
HOOLIGAN HOVEL? IT'S REALLY SORT OF QUAINT WHEN YOU THINK ABOUT IT.
WE'LL SEE HOW QUAINT YOU THINK THEY ARE WHEN THEY'RE MANIPULATING YOUR EMOTIONS, OR EVEN BETTER, SPITTING ON YOU.
OH, YOU'VE GOTTA BE KIDDING ME.
WELL, NOW IT ALL BEGINS TO MAKE SENSE.

SORRY, THE DOORS DON'T OPEN 'TIL TEN. DON'T THINK OUR PREVIOUS ACQUAINTANCE GIVES YOU SPECIAL PRIVILEGES.
LOOK, MORON. JUST 'CAUSE ROAD RUNNER NEVER GOT AROUND TO KICKING THE COYOTE'S BUTT, DON'T THINK YOU CAN KEEP COMING BACK HERE AND MESSING WITH MY TOWN.
ETHAN, REALLY. SUCH CRASS COMMERCIALISM. WHATEVER HAPPENED TO THE DREAMS YOU HAD? YOU WERE GOING TO BE A LORD OF CHAOS. NOW LOOK AT YOU.
I'VE BEGUN A NEW CHAPTER IN MY LIFE, RUPERT. I'M A LEGITIMATE BUSINESSMAN NOW, AND GROWING QUITE WEALTHY, THANK YOU.
THERE'S NOTHING LEGITIMATE ABOUT YOU. AND IF YOU'RE WEALTHY, IT'S 'CAUSE YOU'RE SELLING MAGIC MORE ADDICTIVE THAN CRACK.
NOW THEN. WHERE ON EARTH DID YOU MANAGE TO FIND AN ENTIRE FAMILY OF BAUMESEL?
I'VE NO IDEA WHAT YOU'RE TALKING ABOUT. I WOULD SUGGEST YOU VACATE THE PREMISES BEFORE I'M FORCED TO CALL ON THE POLICE.

BAP
WRONG ANSWER.
SHALL WE BEGIN AGAIN? I'M NOT SURE HOW LONG I CAN CONTROL HER.
YES, AND YOU'RE DOING AN EXCELLENT JOB THUS FAR.
THE FIRST THING YOU MUST UNDERSTAND IS THAT THEY CAME TO ME.
THEY NEEDED TO RE-ESTABLISH A FOOTHOLD ON THIS PLANE, AND QUICKLY. IN EXCHANGE FOR MY ASSISTANCE, THEY WOULD MAKE ME DISGUSTINGLY RICH.
THEY'RE ALONE, YOU SEE. THEIR MOTHER IS STILL TRAPPED ON THE OTHER SIDE.
WHERE?

"THERE'S A CLEARING IN MILLER'S WOODS. IN THE MIDDLE OF IT IS A LARGE TREE. A VERY OLD TREE. A VERY OLD TREE. BENEATH IT, THERE'S A HOLE INTO THIS WORLD.
"SMALL ENOUGH FOR MY LITTLE HOOLIGAN FRIENDS, BUT NOT BIG ENOUGH FOR DEAR OLD MUM.
"THEY'VE BEEN STEALING SPECIAL THINGS TO WHICH THEIR OWNERS ARE EMOTIONALLY ATTACHED. THERE'S POWER IN THAT.
"THEY BRING THESE LITTLE TRINKETS TO MOTHER AS TRIBUTE. SOMEHOW, THEY CAN DRAIN OFF THE RESIDUAL ENERGIES IMBUED IN THESE OBJECTS AND GIVE IT TO THEIR MOTHER.
"SHE'S USING THAT POWER TO WIDEN THE HOLE.
"BUT THE STOLEN THINGS ALSO GIVE HER A CONNECTION TO THE OWNERS. AND WHEN SHE PASSES OVER INTO THIS WORLD, SHE'S PLANNING TO EAT EVERY LAST ONE OF THEM."
NOW HERE'S SOMETHING YOU DON'T SEE EVERY DAY.
YES, WELL, CLEARLY WE'VE STUMBLED UPON A MAGICAL NEXUS OF SOME SORT.
YUP. MAGIC TREE.
MAKES YOU WONDER JUST HOW MANY OF 'EM THERE ARE.
NOW THERE'S A THOUGHT I'D RATHER NOT HAVE. THOUGH YOU'D THINK WITH SO MANY THEY COULD KEEP THE PLACE A LITTLE CLEANER.

HUJIXCL YJEQOPL FXUVPUYL!
HUJIXCL YJEQOPL FXUVPUYL!
HUJIXCL YJEQOPL FXUVPUYL!
AAAHHHH YAHHH!
HUJIXCL YJEQOPL FXUVPUYL!
HUJIXCL YJEQOPL FXUVPUYL!
Y'KNOW, NOT THAT IT ISN'T A HEARTWARMING SPRINGER MOMENT TO SEE A MOTHER REUNITED WITH HER KIDS...
...BUT YOU AND YOUR LITTLE THIEVES DON'T BELONG HERE.

YEEE-ARRR!
...YYEEE-ARRRR...
HEY, OZ... WHY DON'T YOU PUT THIS SOMEWHERE SO IT DOESN'T GET BROKEN.
LOOK! PEZ WITCH!
YOU LITTLE MONSTERS! GET OFF ME. I SEE MY GUCCI BAG OVER THERE! I WAS WONDERING WHAT HAPPENED TO THAT.
I DIDN'T REALIZE THERE'D BE SO MANY OF THEM IN A SINGLE NEST.
YEAH. FASCINATING.
YAHHR

DON'T GET SO EXCITED. OU'RE NOT STAYING LONG!
DWOANNGG
SORRY, OZ... I'M BEING AS GENTLE AS I CAN.
GHURRKKK!

GRRRRR
GILES, WILLOW, BETTER GET THAT MOJO READY.
ALL RIGHT, GUYS. THIS IS HOW IT'S GONNA BE. WE ALL KNOW WHEN YOUR MOM COMES AROUND, SHE'S GONNA HAVE A SERIOUS MAD-ON, AND I'M GONNA HAVE TO DEAL WITH IT.
I DON'T THINK YOU WANT THAT. FRANKLY, I CAN DO WITHOUT IT, TOO.
LAST THING I NEED IS A TOWN SWARMING WITH FURRY LITTLE ORPHANS WITH SHARP TEETH AND STICKY FINGERS. SO HERE'S THE DEAL--
YOU CAN STAY, AND THINGS GET MESSY. OR YOU CAN TAKE YOUR MOM AND GO BACK WHERE YOU BELONG.
WHAT'S IT GONNA BE?
!
!

HO-HUM.
YAHHH.
SPIRITS OF EARTH AND WOOD, WE INVOKE THEE, WITH ALL DUE PRAISE AND SUPPLICATION.
WITH NURTURING SOIL, AND STRENGTH OF WOOD, WE HEAL NOW THIS WOUND ON THE BODY OF OUR WORLD.
HEY, WAIT A MINUTE, YOU.
I THINK THAT BELONGS TO ME.
WITH THE POWER OF THE SPIRITS OF EARTH AND WOOD...
...WE HEAL NOW THIS WOUND, WE BIND THIS BREACH...
GRRRR...
...WE CLOSE THIS DOOR FOREVERMORE.

Y'KNOW, I THINK ONE OF THOSE LITTLE MONKEYS STOLE MY LIPSTICK.
:ahem: MIGHT I SUGGEST WE TAKE OUR LEAVE BEFORE WHATEVER MAGICS ARE AFFECTING THIS PLACE BEGIN TO WEAR OFF?
SO YOUR FAVORITE PLAYMATE IS GONE. I GUESS WE COULDN'T EXPECT HIM TO WAIT FOR US TO DEAL WITH THE BIG EVIL FIRST.
YES, WELL, I THINK WE CAN BE FAIRLY CERTAIN THAT WE HAVEN'T SEEN THE LAST OF ETHAN RAYNE. FRANKLY I WONDER IF HE ISN'T BEGINNING TO ENJOY YOUR BEATINGS.
GREAT. THANKS FOR THE NAUSEA.
FOR RENT
CLOSED
NO, REALLY. I DON'T KNOW WHY YOU ALL GOT SO WRAPPED UP IN THAT HOOLIGAN THING. NO SELF-CONTROL. IT'S LIKE, THE LATEST CRAZE COMES ALONG, AND YOU ALL GET WACKY.
IT'S SAD. WE'RE JUST SO WEAK.
YES, WELL, PERHAPS WE'VE ALL LEARNED A LESSON ABOUT ENVY AND PEER PRESSURE.
PLEASE. WHAT PLANET ARE *YOU* FROM? WHAT I'VE LEARNED IS THAT IF EVERYONE HAD LISTENED TO ME IN THE FIRST PLACE, ALL WOULD HAVE BEEN RIGHT WITH THE WORLD.
I SUPPOSE IT WAS TOO MUCH TO HOPE THAT THIS EXPERIENCE HAD ACTUALLY TAUGHT HER SOMETHING.
YUP.

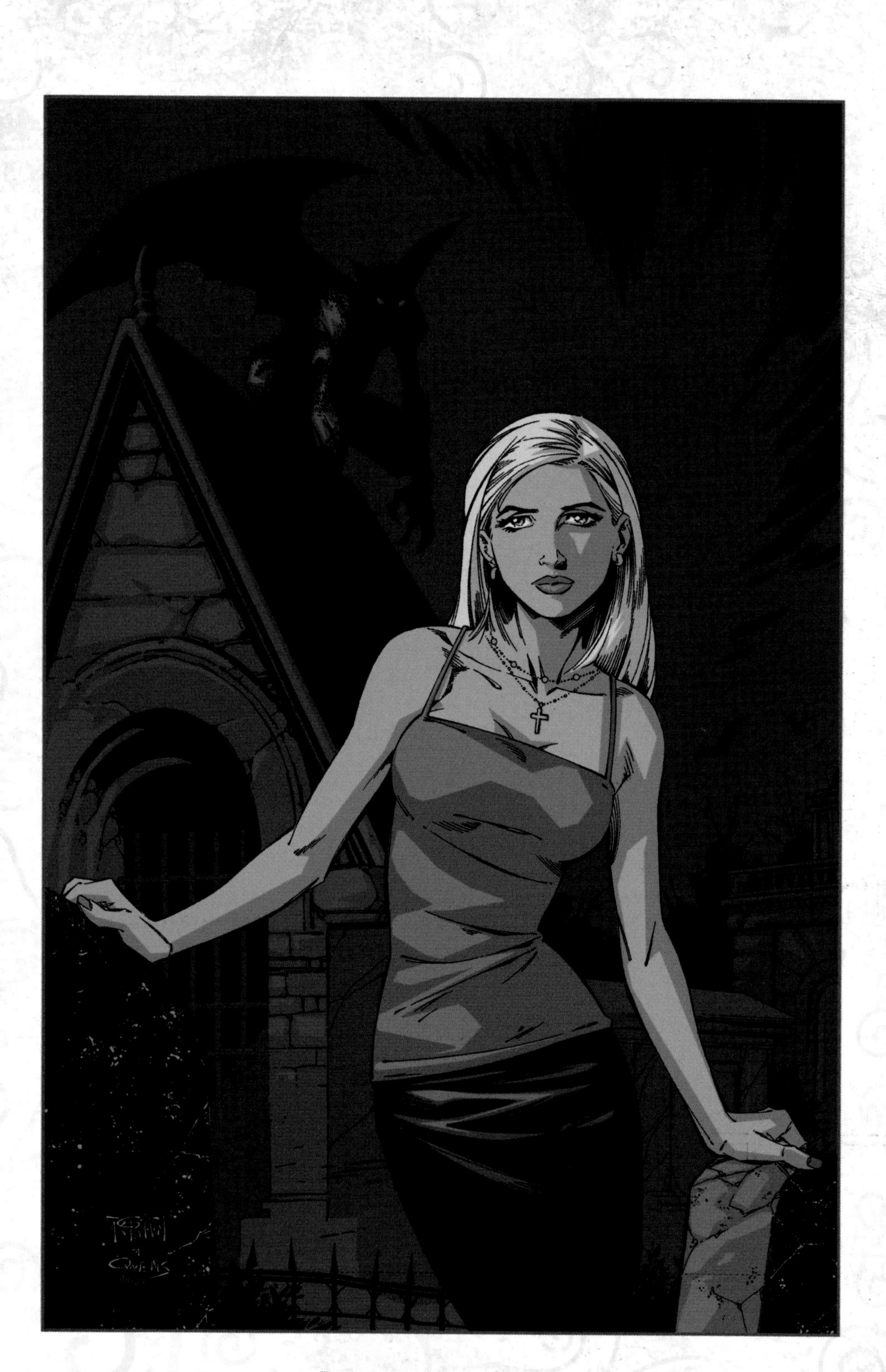

Art by Randy Green *with* Andy Owens *and* Guy Major

BAD DOG

EAT WOOD, LOSER!

"EAT WOOD"? WHAT KIND OF PHRASE IS--
KA-PLINK
OH PLEASE, GIVE ME A BREAK. I'M A SLAYER, NOT A STAND-UP.
STILL, YOU GOTTA ADMIT...
CATCHPHRASE-WISE? HE'S GOT A POINT. I MEAN, "EAT WOOD"? WHERE'S THE POETRY?
SUNNYDALE CEMETERY
OKAY, MAYBE IT LACKS THE WIT OF, SAY, "IT'S CLOBBERIN' TIME." BUT NO FAIR. THAT'S A CLASSIC. OW!
ARE YOU HURT?
IT'S NOTHING.
I WORRY ABOUT YOU. AND I WANTED TO SEE YOU, TO CHECK ON YOU, BEFORE...
BEFORE WHAT?

"OH."
SUNNYDALE CEMETERY
"YOU EVER WANT A NORMAL LIFE?"
IF BY "NORMAL" YOU MEAN A LIFE WITHOUT MYSTERY MEAT? COUNT ME IN.
WHAT DO YOU MEAN?
YEAH, YOU'RE TALKING TO THE SCOOBY GANG, HERE. "NORMAL" FOR US HAS MORE THAN THE USUAL LOOP-HOLES.
I MEAN NORMAL, LIKE, A BOYFRIEND WHO'S NOT SUCH A... A HYPHENATE. AS IN BOYFRIEND-HYPHEN-VAMPIRE.
OR MAYBE, BOYFRIEND-HYPHEN-WEREWOLF.
NO, OZ, I DIDN'T MEAN...
BUFFY, SOME GIRLS LIKE HAVING THEIR FELLAS HYPHENATED. LIKE BOYFRIEND-HYPHEN-GUITARIST-HYPHEN-GENIUS-HYPHEN-SNUGGLE-BUNNY...
AND SUDDENLY, LUNCH'S NOT THE MOST NAUSEATING THING IN THE ROOM.

UH, GUYS? YOU KNOW THAT I WAS TALKING ABOUT ME, RIGHT?
SURE, IT'S JUST...
HAVE YOU SEEN A LUNAR CHART LATELY? THAT TIME OF THE MONTH.
BUT I WAS ONLY-- OH!
HEY! HI! YOU'RE BUFFY, RIGHT? ALAN DUFFY, AND I WANTED TO TALK TO YOU. I HEAR YOU GUYS ARE...
BUMP
...BLOWING ME OFF. HMPH!
THAT NIGHT.
YOU THINK MAYBE BUFFY WAS RIGHT? AND THE STRAIGHTS ARE HAVING MORE FUN? BECAUSE BETWEEN YOU AND ME, OZ...
I JUST HATE LOCKING YOU UP LIKE AN ANIMAL.
IF IT MAKES YOU FEEL BETTER, IT'S NO BARGAIN ON THIS SIDE OF THE BARS. BUT THREE DAYS A MONTH, WE CAN DEAL. YOU'D BETTER STEP BACK NOW, I CAN FEEL THE CHANGE...

STARTING TO...
RRRAARG-H
RIGHT. I'M GLAD WE GOT THIS CHANCE TO TALK. SIGH
JUNK FOOD--CHECK. CDS--CHECK. TRASHY MAGAZINES--CHECK. NO DOUBT, THIS IS A WORLD-CLASS WEREWOLF-SITTER'S CARE PACKAGE.
JUST HOPE IT CAN REMOVE THE TASTE OF FOOT FROM MY MOUTH. HEY, WILLOW?
WILLOW!

TWENTY MINUTES LATER.
THE GUN HASN'T BEEN FIRED. IF THERE WAS A STRUGGLE, IT WAS BRIEF.
HE SURPRISED HER.
SOME-THING DID.
WHAT'S THAT SUPPOSED TO MEAN?
MERELY THAT WE CAN'T ASSUME ANYTHING.
OH YEAH? HOW ABOUT ASSUMING OZ COULD BE KILLING WILLOW RIGHT NOW? WE GOTTA HUNT HIM DOWN.
AND D
WHAT
KILL HIM?
YEAH! IF WE HAVE TO!
TWENTY-EIGHT DAYS A MONTH HE'S STILL A HUMAN BEING, XANDER!
WELCOME TO DAY TWENTY-NINE.
QUIET! BOTH OF YOU! WILLOW IS SOMEWHERE OUT THERE AND YOU WANT TO TALK ABOUT KILLING?
TALK TO ME WHEN I GET BACK.

GREAT. THESE TRACKS *WOULD* LEAD INTO THE WOODS. WILLOW'S NO AMATEUR. IF OZ TOOK HER, IT MEANS HE'S FASTER, DEADLIER THAN...
SNAP
GOTCHA!
UH... DON'T SHOOT?
WHAT ARE YOU DOING HERE?
GILES FILLED ME IN. THOUGHT I COULD HELP.
BY GETTING YOURSELF SHOT? IF I DIDN'T HAVE SLAYER REFLEXES, YOU'D BE TRANQUILIZED, I'D HAVE TO BABYSIT, AND WILLOW MIGHT BE DEAD. DO ME A FAVOR. GO HOME.
THE WEREWOLF'S A NIGHT CREATURE, BUFFY. LIKE ME. I KNOW HOW IT THINKS. AND HOW TO TRACK IT. YOU WANT TO LET ME HELP, OR WOULD YOU RATHER POUT LIKE A SCHOOL GIRL?

THAT IS SUCH A CHEAP SHOT. I KNOW I'M NOT SOME GROOVY MYSTERIOUS "NIGHT CREATURE" WHO ABANDONS HER FRIENDS EVERY TIME THE SUN SHINES. SO EXCUSE ME FOR BEING NORMAL.
NORMAL? WHAT DOES THAT MEAN?
I DON'T KNOW. NORMAL IS... GOING ON DATES WHEN THE WORLD'S NOT ASLEEP. AND SUN-LIGHT. AND BEING HUMAN, HAVING A LIFE, WEARING KHAKI PANTS, AND--
WAIT!
RUSTLE
OKAY I'M NOT SURE ABOUT THE KHAKIS PART, BUT--
SKRAASHH

SMA-KAASH
SKASH!
WHOMP!
RRRAARGH!

BUFFY, MOVE!
DAMN! CAN'T GET OFF A CLEAN--
FWACK!
UNGH!
THWAP!
LET'S END THIS...

NOW!
THUNK
THWOK
YOU OKAY?
BETTER THAN OZ.
THIS THING ISN'T OZ.
WHERE ARE YOU GOING?
HUNTING. THAT "THING" YOU JUST WHACKED STILL HAD SOME OZ LEFT IN HIM, BUFFY. MIGHT HAVE LED US TO WILLOW. I'LL FIND HER ON MY OWN.
HMMM...
LATER.
OKAY, PUPPY, I GOT THE HIGH VOLTAGE STUN GUN, SO RISE AND SHINE, BUTTERCUP...
GOOD DOGGIE. LET'S GO FOR A WALK.
SNIFF
SNIFF

YOU SMELL SOMETHING, BOY?
I'LL TAKE IT THAT'S LASSIE FOR "YES."
Whimper
THE SEWER. GREAT.
COULDN'T SHE JUST BE TRAPPED DOWN A WELL? NOT THAT I'M COMPLAINING...
SPLASH
DEAD END. OKAY, NOW I'M COMPLAINING. BUT YOU STILL SMELL SOMETHING, OKAY...
BUT IF ALL YOU'RE AFTER IS SOME WEREWOLF CHOW, I'VE GOT A ROLLED-UP NEWSPAPER WITH YOUR NAME ON IT...
THE SLAYER!

OZ, NO! IT'S ALMOST...
SNAP
RRARR!
POW
...DAYLIGHT.
THE NIGHT HAS PASSED-- MY SPELL IS COMPLETE! THE WITCH'S POWER IS MINE! I'M READY...
... FOR THE TRANSFORMATION...

...TO MY HIGHER SELF!
CAN YOU GET WILLOW OUT OF HERE?
ON IT.
DO IT. I'LL TAKE CARE OF THE AMAZING SPIDER-BOY HERE.
I'M DOUBTING IT, SLAYER. I'VE BEEN PRACTICING THE DEADLIEST MAGIC SINCE FOURTH GRADE. DRAINING THE WICCA GAVE ME POWER-- AND I PLAN TO USE IT!
HE'S A TOTAL NUT-JOB.
I'M GETTING THAT.
BUFFY!
GO!

NOT TO GET TOO PERSONAL HERE, ALAN, BUT WHAT EXACTLY IS YOUR DAMAGE? YOU ACTUALLY WANT TO BE A MUTANT?
YES! DUH! YOU THINK ANYONE IN THIS SCHOOL WOULD EVER PAY ATTENTION TO NORMAL LITTLE ALAN DUFFY?!? NO!!!
I WANT POWER!
I WANT ATTENTION!
I WANT RESPECT!
NOOOOO!
YUCK.

WHAM

HEH.

ANGEL?

I'VE DECIDED...

...NORMAL'S OVERRATED.

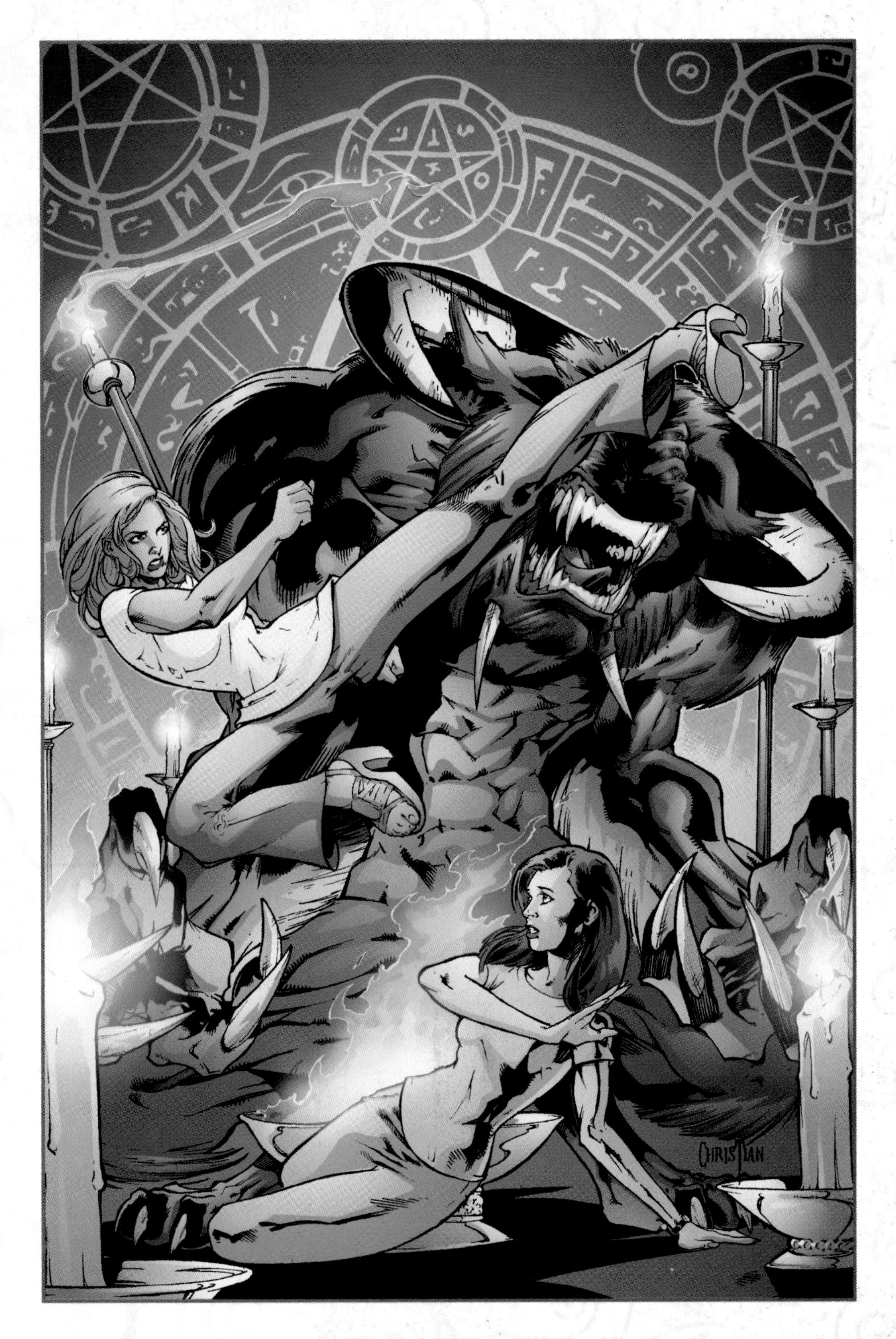

Art by christian zanier with guy major

FOOD CHAIN PART 2

THERE'S A CERTAIN SPARKLE TO SOUTHERN CALIFORNIA. OR , AT LEAST, TO THE MYTH IT HAS BECOME IN AMERICAN POP CULTURE.
THE PERFECT WEATHER, THE PERFECTLY P.C. POLITICS, THE PERFECT TANS AND PERFECT TEETH. BUT SCRATCH THE SURFACE, AND SOME THINGS ARE JUST AS TRUE HERE AS THEY ARE EVERYWHERE ELSE.
SUNNYDALE, CALIFORNIA, JUST FOR INSTANCE, CERTAINLY HAS ITS SHARE OF GUYS LIKE THIS. THEY'RE THE BOTTOM-FEEDERS OF THE FOOD CHAIN, BUT SOMEHOW, THEY NEVER STARVE.
WHAT DO YOU THINK YOU'RE DOIN', PUKE? YOU DON'T ASK MY GIRL TO THE MOVIES. YOU GOT A LESSON COMIN'!
BRAD, DON'T!
WHAT'S WRONG WITH YOU, SUZE? WE HAD SOMETHING GOING, AND YOU GO OUT WITH THIS LITTLE RUNT?
GO TO HELL. OH, WOW, WHAT BRAVE BOYS YOU ARE. YOU'RE, WHAT, FIVE AGAINST ONE? PLEASE. GO BE NEANDERTHALS ON YOUR OWN TIME, ALL RIGHT? I'M ON A DATE.
YEAH, Y' KNOW WHAT? I'M GONE. ENJOY LIFE WITH THE LOSERS.
EXIT
YEAH. WORDS FOR YOU TO LIVE BY.
YEP. BOTTOM-FEEDERS GET PLENTY TO EAT, BUT THEY'RE USUALLY NONE TOO BRIGHT--ALMOST ALWAYS THE LAST TO LEARN ONE OF THE PRIMARY LESSONS OF THE FOOD CHAIN.
A CERTAIN JEDI MASTER PROBABLY SAID IT BEST...
...THERE'S ALWAYS A BIGGER FISH.

SCHOOL BUS
DO NOT PASS
...I MEAN, ALL I WANTED WAS A LITTLE HABITRAIL, NOTHING TOO EXPENSIVE.
YOUR MOM DIDN'T GO FOR IT, HUH?
SHE SAID HABITRAILS ARE FOR GERBILS, NOT RATS.
I'M JUST TRYING TO GIVE AMY A LITTLE CHANGE OF SCENERY, BUT SUDDENLY MOM'S ALL PET-PREJUDICED.
MAYBE YOU COULD CALL THE ASPCA?
XANDER! GO LONG!
SEE THAT? I'M NOT TURNIN' THIS TIME, LADIES. I'VE LEARNED. COMES A TIME WHEN EVEN CHARLIE BROWN WON'T FALL FOR LUCY'S FOOTBALL TRICK. NOW IS THE--
WHUFFFFFF!
THUNKK!
OUCH. Y'KNOW, I'M SERIOUSLY CONSIDERING TAKING THIS AS A BAD OMEN. WINDS OF FATE, ALL THAT. FEEL FREE TO TALK ME OUT OF IT.

HEY, MASHAD! GOOD ARM!
WHY I OUGHTA...
Y'KNOW, XANDER, IF THAT'S HOW YOU START YOUR DAY, IT CAN ONLY GET BETTER, RIGHT?
I GUESS YOU'RE RIGHT, BUFFY. GOTTA LOOK ON THE BRIGHT SIDE.
I MEAN, I COULD HAVE HAD MY HEAD TORN OFF MY BODY LAST NIGHT LIKE ARTIE POLK. IN THAT LIGHT, TODAY SEEMS ALL SHINY AND NEW.
HEAD... TORN OFF... SIGH. SO MUCH FOR HANGING AT THE BRONZE TONIGHT.
THINK OF IT THIS WAY, BUFFY --IF THAT'S HOW YOU START YOUR DAY, IT CAN ONLY GET BETTER, RIGHT?
"SADLY, I'M GUESSING IT GETS MUCH WORSE FROM HERE."
I APPRECIATE YOU GUYS COMING DOWN HERE WITH ME, BUT REALLY, I CAN MANAGE THE CLUE-HUNTING THING JUST FINE. YOU SHOULD GO TO A MOVIE. HAVE FUN.
OR WE COULD, Y'KNOW, NOT. OKAY, IT'S NOT THE BRONZE, BUT THIS RESEMBLES FUN IN A WAY. HANGING OUT WITH FRIENDS ON FRIDAY NIGHT, INVESTIGATING A DECAPITATION.

IT'S EVEN ROMANTIC IN A WAY. IF YOU LEAVE OUT THAT DECAPITATION PART.
EXIT
SO, WHAT ARE WE LOOKING FOR, ANYWAY? BIGFOOT PRINTS? DEMON SPOOR?
I DON'T KNOW. ANYTHING. SOMETHING THE POLICE WOULDN'T NOTICE. OR WOULDN'T HAVE BEEN LOOKING FOR.
THAT'S WEIRD. IT'S LIKE THEY DIDN'T FINISH THE OUTLINE.
POLICE
YEAH. THEY DID.
LOOKS LIKE WHATEVER GOT ARTIE DIDN'T STOP WITH HIS HEAD.
UNLESS... HIS HEAD WAS LAST. WHICH WOULD MEAN HE COULDA BEEN ALIVE WHEN... I SHOULD SHUT UP NOW.
WE'RE NOT GONNA FIND ANYTHING HERE. THE COPS HAVE BEEN OVER THIS PLACE. I DON'T KNOW WHAT I WAS THINKING.
PROBABLY THAT IF WE POKED AROUND THE MURDER SCENE, MAYBE THE MONSTER WOULD COME AFTER US, AND THEN YOU COULD KILL IT. WHICH, COME TO THINK OF IT, IS A VERY BAD PLAN.

"THAT WASN'T THE PLAN, WILL. BUT IT DOESN'T LOOK LIKE WE'RE GONNA GET THAT LUCKY TONIGHT."
"HELLO? BUFFY? MAYBE THIS IS A GOOD TIME TO MENTION... DECAPITATION? NOT MY IDEA OF GETTING LUCKY."
"GOTTA TELL YA, XAND, I'D BE AFRAID TO ASK WHAT IS."
PLEASE ALLOW ME
TO INTRODUCE MYSELF
I'M A MAN
KLANK
SHRRPT
OF WEALTH
AND TASTE

HHUNNFFF!
CLOSE ONE, BOYS. I'M ALMOST SORRY WE HAVE TO BEAT YOU AGAIN.
NOT THIS TIME, SUMMERS-- I WOULDN'T CELEBRATE VICTORY JUST YET.
SPAKK!
HOW 'BOUT NOW?
GOOD A TIME AS ANY.
GOTTA SAY, THERE'S SOMETHING YOU DON'T SEE EVERY DAY.

I DIDN'T THINK GILES EVEN KNEW HIS WAY TO THE BEACH.
APPARENTLY HE'S DECEIVED US ALL. THIS IS A PLACE OF FUN, RIGHT? NORMALLY SUCH THINGS ARE GOOD FOR GILES PREVENTION.
MAYBE HE'S LOST?
IF NOT, WE COULD *HELP* HIM.
SORRY TO INTERRUPT YOUR GAME, BUT THERE'S WORK TO BE DONE. ANOTHER ATTACK LAST NIGHT, APPARENTLY BY THE SAME CREATURE.
GREAT. THANKS FOR THE UPDATE. AND THIS CAN'T WAIT FOR TONIGHT'S PATROL... WHY, EXACTLY?
THE BOY KILLED LAST NIGHT WAS DOUGLAS RYAN. BOTH HE AND ARTHUR POLK WERE MEMBERS OF THE CULT OF YLISANDROTH. IT SEEMS LIKELY THE OTHER MEMBERS ARE IN DANGER.
NO. WAIT. WE SHOULD TAKE A VOTE. I MEAN, WE'RE GOING TO BLOW A DAY OF FUN IN THE SUN TO BABYSIT A BUNCH OF GUYS WE HATE?
DON'T YOU THINK HATE'S A LITTLE STRONG?
CAN WE JUST GET OUR STUFF?

THERE ARE WORSE THINGS TO DO ON A BEAUTIFUL SATURDAY THAN HANG OUT IN HAMMERSMITH PARK.
USED TO BE, BRAD CAUFIELD AND HIS FRIENDS WOULD HAVE BEEN OUT RAISING HELL RIGHT NOW. THEY'VE DONE SOME PRETTY BAD THINGS, TRUTH BE TOLD.
WORSHIPPING THE DEMON YLISANDROTH, FOR INSTANCE. THAT WAS BAD *AND* STUPID. YLISANDROTH ONLY WANTED THEM AROUND SO SHE COULD LEECH THEIR LIFE FORCES FOR HERSELF.
SHE HAD PLANNED TO SACRIFICE THEM TO THE ELDER DEMON THAT *SHE* WORSHIPPED, BUT THE SLAYER PUT A STOP TO ALL THAT. YLISANDROTH WASN'T VERY NICE.
BUT THEN, NEITHER ARE BRAD AND HIS BUDS. THEY LEARNED A LESSON, BUT THEY'RE ALREADY STARTING TO FORGET. AFTER ALL, THEY DID SOME VERY NASTY THINGS, AND LIVED TO TELL ABOUT IT.
UNTIL RECENTLY.
THERE ARE WORSE THINGS TO DO ON A BEAUTIFUL SATURDAY THAN HANG OUT IN HAMMERSMITH PARK. FOR INSTANCE...
XANDER WAS RIGHT. WE DON'T EVEN LIKE THESE GUYS. HERE THEY'RE HAVING A GREAT TIME, AND WE'RE STUCK DOING NOTHING BUT WATCHING THEM PLAY FRISBEE.
THEY'RE NOT VERY GOOD AT IT, THOUGH. THAT'S A COMFORT.

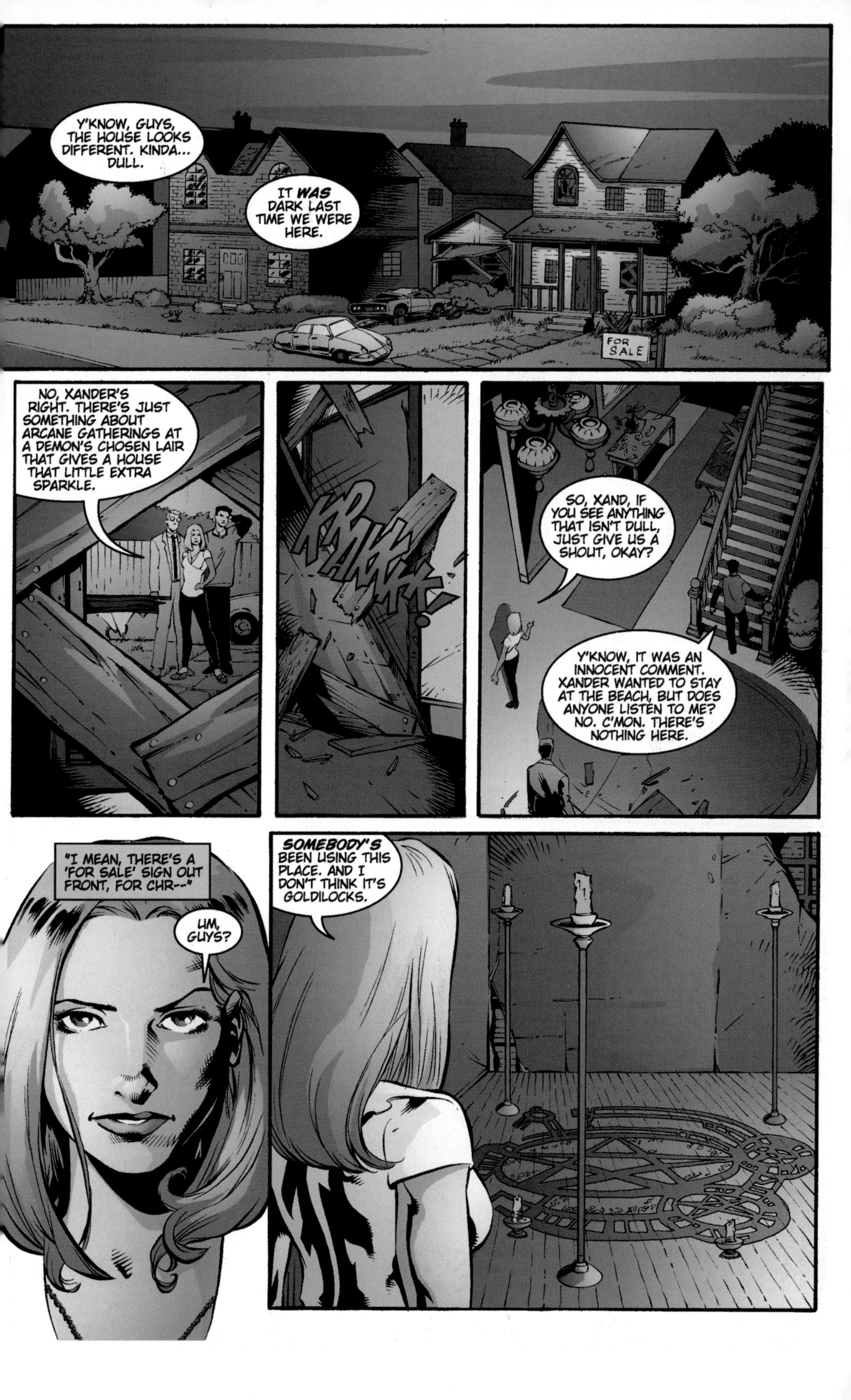
Y'KNOW, GUYS, THE HOUSE LOOKS DIFFERENT. KINDA... DULL.
IT *WAS* DARK LAST TIME WE WERE HERE.
FOR SALE
NO, XANDER'S RIGHT. THERE'S JUST SOMETHING ABOUT ARCANE GATHERINGS AT A DEMON'S CHOSEN LAIR THAT GIVES A HOUSE THAT LITTLE EXTRA SPARKLE.
KRAKKK!
SO, XAND, IF YOU SEE ANYTHING THAT ISN'T DULL, JUST GIVE US A SHOUT, OKAY?
Y'KNOW, IT WAS AN INNOCENT COMMENT. XANDER WANTED TO STAY AT THE BEACH, BUT DOES ANYONE LISTEN TO ME? NO. C'MON. THERE'S NOTHING HERE.
"I MEAN, THERE'S A 'FOR SALE' SIGN OUT FRONT, FOR CHR--"
UM, GUYS?
SOMEBODY'S BEEN USING THIS PLACE. AND I DON'T THINK IT'S GOLDILOCKS.

"WHAT DO YOU THINK, GILES? AFTER WHAT I DID TO YLISANDROTH, I THOUGHT--"
"NO. YLISANDROTH IS DEAD. BUT, CLEARLY, WHOEVER OR WHATEVER IS KILLING THESE BOYS HAS A CONNECTION TO HER, AND BY EXTENSION, TO THEIR NOW-DEFUNCT CULT...
"...IN FACT, IT MAY EVEN BE ONE OF THESE BOYS. THE SAVAGERY OF THESE KILLINGS--PERHAPS THEY'VE CALLED SOMETHING UP FROM BEYOND."
"AND NOW IT'S KILLING THEM. GREAT. I GUESS I KNOW HOW WE'LL ALL BE SPENDING THE NIGHT."
STOP JOSTLING. DON'T DRAW ATTENTION TO THE CAR.
THIS WASN'T MY IDEA. HOW WAS I TO HAVE KNOWN CONNOR WOULD BRING HIS DATE UP HERE?
HOW WERE YOU TO--OH GOD, THIS IS A NIGHTMARE, ISN'T IT? PLEASE, WHY CAN'T I WAKE UP? UNLESS IT'S HELL. THAT'S IT. I COULD BE IN HELL. WHICH WOULD EXPLAIN A LOT.

WHAT'S UP WITH YOU, BUDDY? YOU THINK I DON'T SEE YOU BACK THERE?
OZ, SLOW DOWN, BRAD'S TURNING!
OKAY, WELL, HE SURE *DRIVES* LIKE A LUNATIC. GOTTA WONDER, THOUGH, IF HE WAS TRYING TO GET AWAY 'CAUSE HE'S GUILTY, OR JUST AFRAID, AFTER WHAT HAPPENED TO ARTIE AND DOUG.
HE'S GONE.

GONE? WHAT DO YOU MEAN, GONE? THAT'S NOT GOOD. SEE, WE SHOULD'VE TAKEN JUSTIN, OR CONNOR.
DO YOU THINK IT GOT HIM? I MEAN, WE WERE RIGHT BEHIND HIM.
-SNIFF- -SNIFF- I DON'T KNOW. THERE'S *SOMETHING*--
BRAHHHRRRR
SOMETHING! THAT'S SOMETHING!
OW!

WHACK
UHNFFF!
OZ? ARE YOU OKAY?
ONLY IF THE WORLD IS SUPPOSED TO BE OUT OF FOCUS.
...HUFF... GOTTA TELL YA... HUFF... JUSTIN... HUFF... YOU LIVE A... HUFF... BORING LIFE... HUFF... BUT THEN... HUFF...WHO AM I... HUFF...
KER-ASSHHH!

GRAWRRR
OKAY, I TAKE IT BACK.
NO, PLEASE, DON'T... PLEASE I...
BRAD? OH, GOD, IT'S YOU--
BACK OFF, FURBALL.
OH, GOD... OH, GOD...
HRRRRMMM
THUD

VVRRRRRRRR
JUSSSSS-TINNNNN...
UNGHHH!
OZ!
THUDDD
SCREECH
OKAY. THAT'S ONE WAY TO FIGHT DEMONS. I ALWAYS SAY, WHATEVER WORKS FOR YOU.
AT LEAST JUSTIN GOT AWAY, BUFFY. WE SORT OF LOST TRACK OF BRAD.

NOT FOR LONG, THOUGH. OZ JUST RAN HIM OVER. NOW WE CAN--
START LOOKING FOR HIM AGAIN. HE CAN'T HAVE GONE FAR, NOT BLEEDING LIKE THAT.
ACTUALLY, I THINK I KNOW JUST WHERE TO LOOK. BUT IF I'M RIGHT, WE'RE GOING TO NEED HELP.
A GOOD SLAYER IS A PREPARED SLAYER.
RRRRINNGG
THANK GOD! CAN WE GO NOW?
SHORTLY...
IF MY SUSPICIONS PROVE CORRECT, WE SHOULD HAVE EVERYTHING NECESSARY FOR--
GILES, COME ON. WE CAN DO INVENTORY ON THE WAY. WE NEED ANYTHING, WE CAN ALWAYS STOP AT WAL-MART.
YES! JUST AS I THOUGHT. "THE DEMON QUAFONGG MAY CONFER UPON ITS WORSHIPPERS THE CURSE OF POWER, CAUSING THEM TO TAKE THE FORM OF HORRIFIC BEASTS."
"QUAFONGG PROMISES WISH FULFILLMENT, BUT IN TRUTH THIS CURSE IS A YOKE FROM MASTER TO SLAVE, PREPARING THE WORSHIPPER'S OWN BODY FOR INHABITATION BY THE DEMON HIMSELF."
"BRAD NEVER WAS VERY BRIGHT."

HEY. HE'S STILL IN THERE. GOT EVERYTHING WE NEED?
I BELIEVE SO-- THOUGH I MUST SAY, I'M STUMPED. AFTER YLISANDROTH'S PROMISES DIDN'T WORK OUT, BRAD MUST HAVE BEEN DESPERATE TO RAISE ANOTHER DEMON IN HER PLACE...
"DESPERATE, AND FOOLISH AS WELL."
OH... PLEASE... YOU'VE GOT TO HELP... I DIDN'T MEAN FOR ANY OF THIS TO HAPPEN. I DIDN'T KNOW IT WOULD BE LIKE THIS.
THEY WERE MY FRIENDS.
NO. QUAFONGG... IS YOUR ONLY FRIEND.
NEVER FORGET THAT YOU CAME TO ME. YOUR MOTHER DYING, WASTING AWAY... YOU THOUGHT THE PRETENDER YLISANDROTH WOULD CURE HER. QUAFONGG CAN SAVE HER, AS PROMISED.
BUT ONLY WHEN YOU HAVE SPILLED THE BLOOD I REQUIRE IN RETURN. TWO YET REMAIN. TWO OF YOUR COMPANIONS.
... NO ... PLEASE, CAN'T WE JUST STOP NOW?
TOO LATE FOR THAT, BOY. THE BLOOD ALREADY STAINS YOUR HANDS. YOU CANNOT GO BACK. AFTER ALL, IF YOU STOP NOW...
...WHAT WILL BECOME OF YOUR MOTHER?

WOW. NOW *THAT* IS REALLY LOW.
WHA--?
NOT THAT WE'RE BUDS OR ANYTHING--NOT EVEN CLOSE, ACTUALLY--BUT USING A GUY'S DYING MOTHER TO MANIPULATE HIM? WITH FRIENDS LIKE YOU, HE COULD USE HIS ENEMIES RIGHT ABOUT NOW.
LET HIM GO.
I THINK NOT.
NOOO!
AS NATURE BURNS, SO DOES MORTAL SPIRIT. THOUGH THE DARKNESS TAKES HOLD, THE SUN MUST RISE. UNTOUCHED, UNTAINTED, UNBOUND.
BRAD, COME ON. FIGHT IT. QUAFONGG DOESN'T HAVE ALL OF YOU YET, OR IT WOULD HAVE TAKEN YOUR BODY FOR ITSELF. SNAP OUT OF IT! YOU DON'T REALLY THINK IT CAN SAVE YOUR MOTHER?
I DON'T THINK HE'S LISTENING.
AH, BUT IT'S AMUSING TO WATCH. BOY? KILL THEM.

THOUGH THE DARKNESS TAKES HOLD, THE SUN MUST RISE. UNTOUCHED, UNTAINTED, UNBOUND!
JUST NOT PAYING ATTENTION.
AIN'T IT ALWAYS THE WAY WITH MONSTERS, THOUGH?
UNTOUCHED, UNTAINTED, UNBOUND!
OZ! NOW!

XANDER, WE'VE GOT TO TRY NOT TO HURT HIM.
I'LL... UGHH... DO MY BEST.
NOOOO! YOU CANNOT!
BUFFY, WAIT! LOOK AT HIM. WE'VE DONE IT. WE'VE SEVERED THE LINK BETWEEN THEM.
HHUNFF
BRAD?
... SO... SORRY...

YOU'LL HAVE PLENTY OF TIME TO BE SORRY. FOR NOW--
--JUST STAY OUT OF THE WAY.
VERMIN! YOU THINK YOU'VE WON? YOU'VE TAKEN MY HOST, BUT AS LONG AS I REMAIN ON THIS PLANE, I STILL HAVE THE POWER TO DESTROY YOU.
DEMONS. THEY HOLD SUCH A GRUDGE.
THING IS, WE TOOK THAT INTO CONSIDERATION.
DIDN'T WE, GUYS?
NO! WHAT HAVE YOU DONE? HOW CAN THIS --

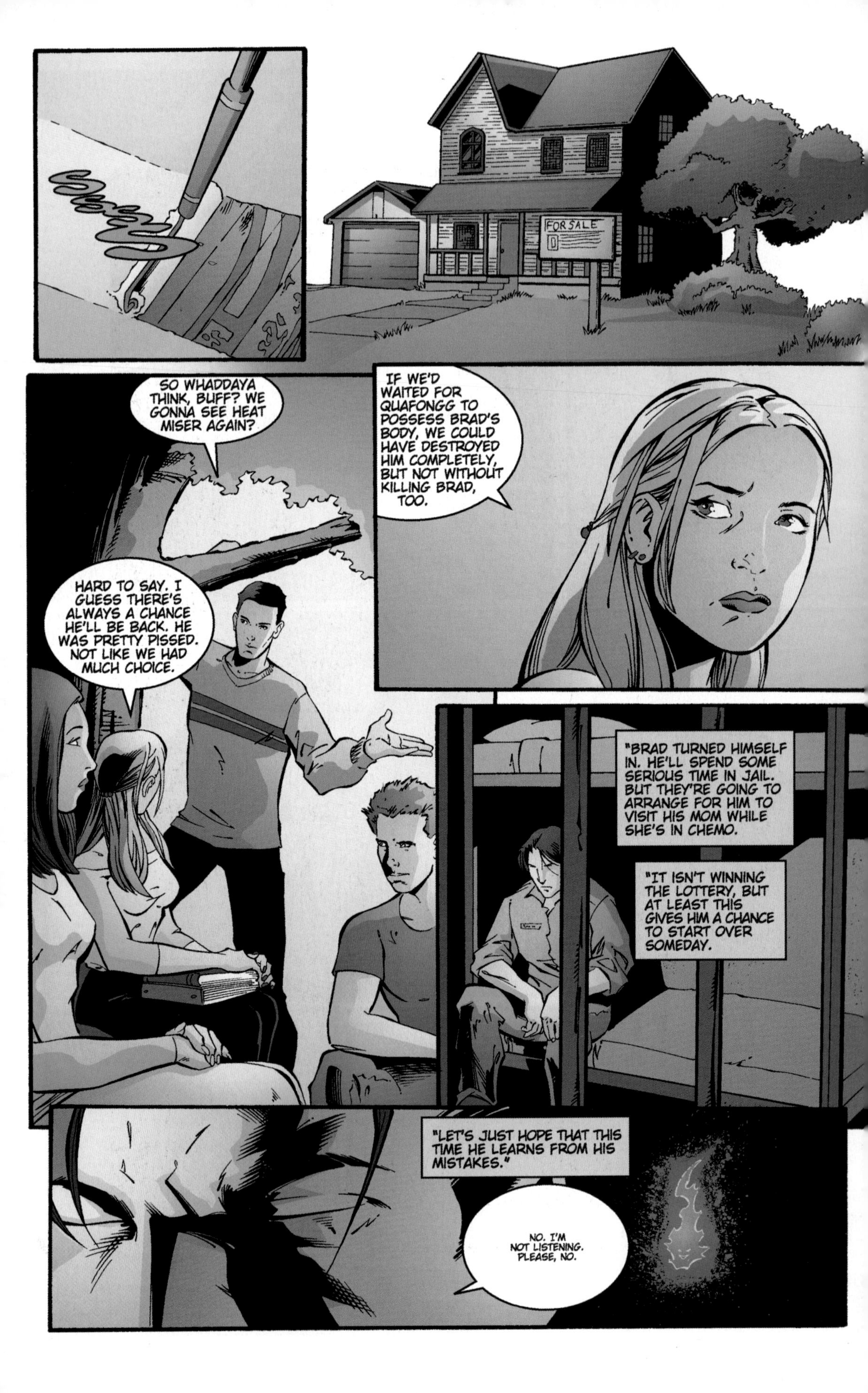

FORSALE
SO WHADDAYA THINK, BUFF? WE GONNA SEE HEAT MISER AGAIN?
IF WE'D WAITED FOR QUAFONGG TO POSSESS BRAD'S BODY, WE COULD HAVE DESTROYED HIM COMPLETELY, BUT NOT WITHOUT KILLING BRAD, TOO.
HARD TO SAY. I GUESS THERE'S ALWAYS A CHANCE HE'LL BE BACK. HE WAS PRETTY PISSED. NOT LIKE WE HAD MUCH CHOICE.
"BRAD TURNED HIMSELF IN. HE'LL SPEND SOME SERIOUS TIME IN JAIL. BUT THEY'RE GOING TO ARRANGE FOR HIM TO VISIT HIS MOM WHILE SHE'S IN CHEMO.
"IT ISN'T WINNING THE LOTTERY, BUT AT LEAST THIS GIVES HIM A CHANCE TO START OVER SOMEDAY.
"LET'S JUST HOPE THAT THIS TIME HE LEARNS FROM HIS MISTAKES."
NO. I'M NOT LISTENING. PLEASE, NO.

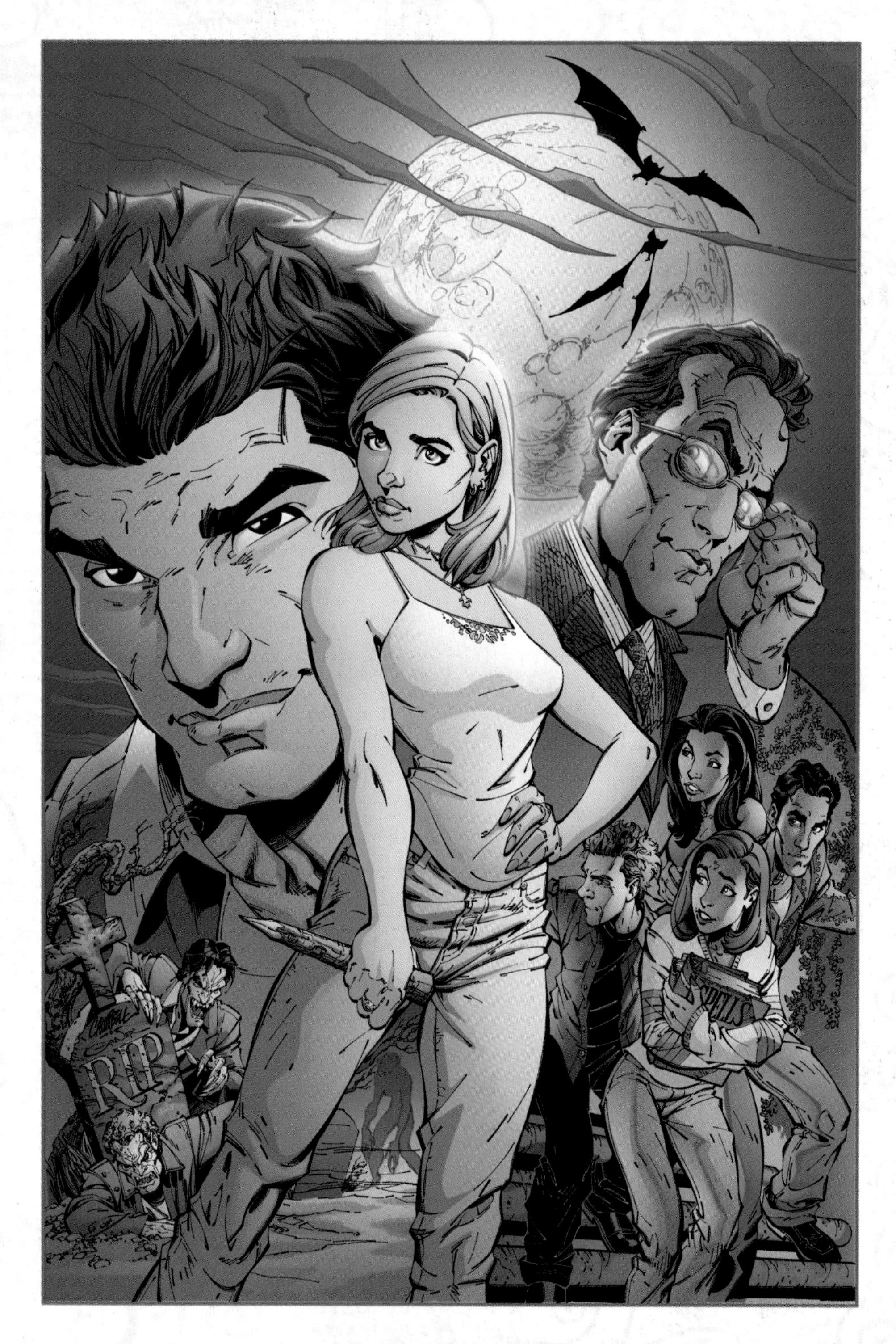

Art by J. Scott Campbell *with* Alex Garner *and* Guy Major

DOUBLE CROSS

GRADUATION DAY, 1999.

THEY THOUGHT IT WAS OVER.
I LOVE WHEN THEY THINK IT'S OVER.
MAKES MY JOB...
SO VERY MUCH...
...EASIER.

AND WHO AM I?
911
YOU KNOW ME.
911
YOU KNOW THAT DARK LITTLE VOICE YOU SOMETIMES HEAR IN THE BACK OF YOUR HEAD?
THE ONE YOU HATE?
THAT'S ME.

I DON'T HAVE A NAME. NOT ONE YOU CAN SPEAK, ANYWAY.
BUT I'VE BEEN AROUND.
WHEREVER THERE IS DEATH...
WHEREVER THERE IS DESPAIR...
I AM THERE TO ASK THE QUESTION...

DO YOU YIELD?
MOST DO. AT THE MOMENT MORTALS SEE DEATH, HOPE CAN BE LOST. HOPE, AND SOMETHING ELSE.
THE SOUL. MEN GIVE THEM UP, YOU SEE.
AND I COLLECT THEM.
SOME ARE WORTH MORE THAN OTHERS. THE MORE I HAVE, THE STRONGER I GET.
AND TONIGHT, TWO SOULS CRY OUT TO BE TAKEN. ALL THEY NEED FROM ME IS A LITTLE... GUIDANCE.

"...Crazy for feelin' so bluuue..."
CLICK
I HATE COUNTRY.
LIKE I NEED HELP FEELING LOUSY. AS IF KILLING A GIANT SNAKE AND FIGHTING A FULL-SCALE VAMP WAR WASN'T ENOUGH. NO, I GOTTA GO ROAD TRIP. GENIUS.
ABSOLUTE GENIUS. WONDER IF THERE'S ANY OF THOSE LITTLE DOUGH-NUTS STILL...
WHOA.
SKREEEE
HI.
YEAH.
LITTLE LATE TO BE OUT ON YOUR OWN, DON'T YOU THINK?
GET IN.
GLAD YOU CAME ALONG WHEN YOU DID.
TROUBLE?
LONG STORY.

MIND IF I CRANK SOME TUNES?
"...for lovin' yooouu..."
I JUST LOVE COUNTRY. YOU?
IT'S ALL RIGHT. IF YOU'RE BROKEN-HEARTED.
AWW. WHAT'S THE MATTER, STUD? YOU BROKEN-HEARTED?
I'LL LIVE.
NOT NECESSARILY.
SKKRRRRCCHH!!

I WONDER WHERE HE IS RIGHT NOW. NOT THAT IT MATTERS
GONE, THAT'S WHERE HE IS.
I THOUGHT KNOWING THIS DAY WAS COMING WOULD MAKE IT HURT LESS. I WAS WRONG.
NEED TIME TO SORT IT ALL OUT. IT'S GOOD TO GET SOME FRESH AIR, AWAY FROM THE SMELL OF SPICY CAJUN SNAKE DEMON. GOOD TO BE...
ALONE?
EVENIN'.

OH. HI. SORRY, I THOUGHT I WAS...
ALONE?
SOMETHING LIKE THAT.
YOU ARE. WE'RE ALL ALONE WHEN YOU GET DOWN TO IT.
THAT'S DEPRESSING.
IT'S LIFE. BUT, YOU ASK ME, IT SURE BEATS THE ALTERNATIVE.
YEAH? WHAT'S THAT?
DEATH.

SHKKSH
VRRM
WHUFF! DON'T KNOW WHO YOU ARE--
BUT I KNOW--
--WHERE YOU'RE GOING!

THUNK!
WHUFF! BUDDY--
--YOU JUST PICKED A REAL BAD NIGHT--
--TO PULL A MORPH 'N' FIGHT ROUTINE.

GRIP... SO TIGHT... LOSING AIR...
NEVER SHOULD HAVE LEFT...
BUFFY.
DO YOU YIELD?

THIS THING'S TOO STRONG...
LOOKS LIKE I PICKED A SWELL TIME TO GET DUMPED...
BYE, ANGEL...
DO YOU YIELD?

DID I MENTION I ENJOY MY WORK?
THIS IS THE PART I LIKE BEST. WATCHING LIFE FLOW OUT OF THEM.
AND YET, FOR ALL THE TIMES I'VE DONE THIS, STILL I WONDER...
WHAT ARE LAST THOUGHTS LIKE?
THIS IS WEIRD...
SNAP!

ANGEL! WHAT ARE YOU DOING HERE?
WISH I KNEW.
YOU GET THE FEELING SOMETHING'S OFF HERE?
ONLY COMPLETELY.
LIKE WE'RE IN A DREAM. LIKE WE'RE SUPPOSED TO... I DUNNO... FIND SOMETHING.
THINK THESE QUALIFY?
BUFFY SUMMERS 1981 – 1999
ANGEL 1753–1999
WE'RE DEAD?
NO...
YOU'RE NOT EVEN HERE.

GREAT. YOU KNOW, I HATE TO SAY IT, BUT I THINK THE TALKING BIRD'S GOT A POINT.
ME TOO. THIS IS JUST A LITTLE TOO TRIPPY TO BE REAL.
SO, THIS IS...WHAT? SOME KIND OF PSYCHIC LINK?
MAYBE. WE'RE DEFINITELY... NOT HERE.
SO WHERE ARE WE?

TOGETHER. I LIKE IT.
SO DO I.
WE'RE DYING.
THIS IS WRONG.
WE HAVE TO BE...
...APART.

DAMN. SO CLOSE.
NO...
KAK

...BUFFY.
NNNGTH!
KRAK

GASP!
NOT ALL OF THEM YIELD.
SOME RUN.
IN THE END, IT MAKES LITTLE DIFFERENCE
SHUNK

SKREEE
BOOM
USUALLY.

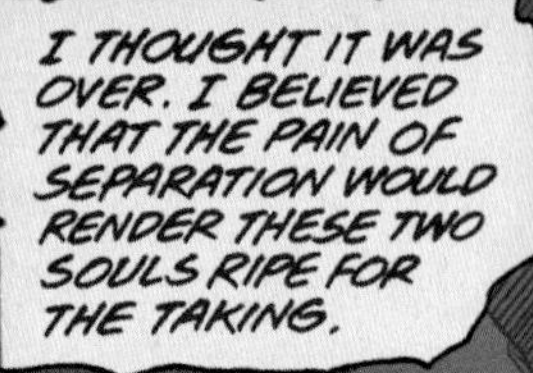
I THOUGHT IT WAS OVER. I BELIEVED THAT THE PAIN OF SEPARATION WOULD RENDER THESE TWO SOULS RIPE FOR THE TAKING.
I WAS WRONG. THOUGH THE TWO LOVERS PART, THEIR CONNECTION REMAINS--AND THAT MAKES THEM STRONG.

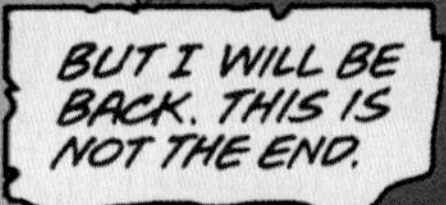
BUT I WILL BE BACK. THIS IS NOT THE END.

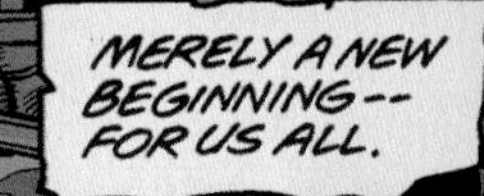
MERELY A NEW BEGINNING--FOR US ALL.

Art by chynna clugston-major *with* guy major

PUNISH ME WITH KISSES

"YOU SEE, THERE'S THIS FLOWER, WILL. THE SNOW FLOWER. IT'S BEAUTIFUL, BRIGHT RED, AND LOOKS LIKE A BURST OF FLAME.
"IT'S RARE, THOUGH, AND IT ONLY GROWS IN NORTHERN CALIFORNIA, AND IT ONLY GROWS IN THE SNOW."
"BECAUSE IT WOULD BE SILLY TO CALL IT THAT IF IT DIDN'T."
"AND THIS ISN'T A SILLY FLOWER. IT'S A GOOD FLOWER. IN FACT, IT'S SO RARE THEY FINE YOU $500 IF THEY CATCH YOU PICKING IT."
Buffy- Please water the plants at least once a day. We'll be back Monday. - W
"SHEESH, TARA. IT BETTER BE SOME FLOWER."
"BUT THERE'S AN EVEN RARER FORM OF IT, WHICH ONLY BLOSSOMS IN THE DAWN OF THE FINAL THAW. ITS PETALS ARE MORE INTRICATE. THEY'RE RED, MOTTLED WITH YELLOW.
"YOU HAVE TO BE THERE RIGHT WHEN IT BLOSSOMS, JUST AS THE SUN TOUCHES IT, IF YOU WANT TO PICK THIS SNOW FLOWER. AS SOON AS THE SUN REACHES FULL BRIGHTNESS, IT WITHERS AND FADES."
GODDARD
SUNNYDALE
152
"SO WE'RE GONNA PICK THIS SPECIAL SNOW FLOWER?"
101
"YES. IF YOU PICK IT AT THE RIGHT MOMENT, IT WON'T WITHER SO FAST. YOU CAN THEN DRY IT AND CRUSH THE PETALS, AND THE POWDER WORKS AS A VITAMIN. IT ENHANCES YOUR SPELL CASTING POWER."
"IT IS A GOOD FLOWER."
"FINAL THAW IS THIS WEEKEND, WILL.
"THERE'S A LITTLE BED AND BREAKFAST OUT NEAR GODDARD.
"IT'S SUPPOSED TO BE WONDERFUL..."
AAAAAAAHHHHHHHH

"...NICE AND QUIET."
I-I-I... THIS IS JUST NOT RIGHT.
I FEEL SO... SO... VIOLATED...
Punish Me With Kisses
WHAT WAS THAT ?
I DON'T KNOW, BUT MY SCOOBY-SENSE IS TINGLING...
...OR SOME-THING.
OHDEAR OHDEAR OHDEAR
COME ON, LET'S CHECK THIS OUT.
OKAY, BUT IF IT TURNS OUT TO BE THAT OLD GUY IN A MONSTER SUIT AGAIN, I'M GOING TO BE VERY UPSET.

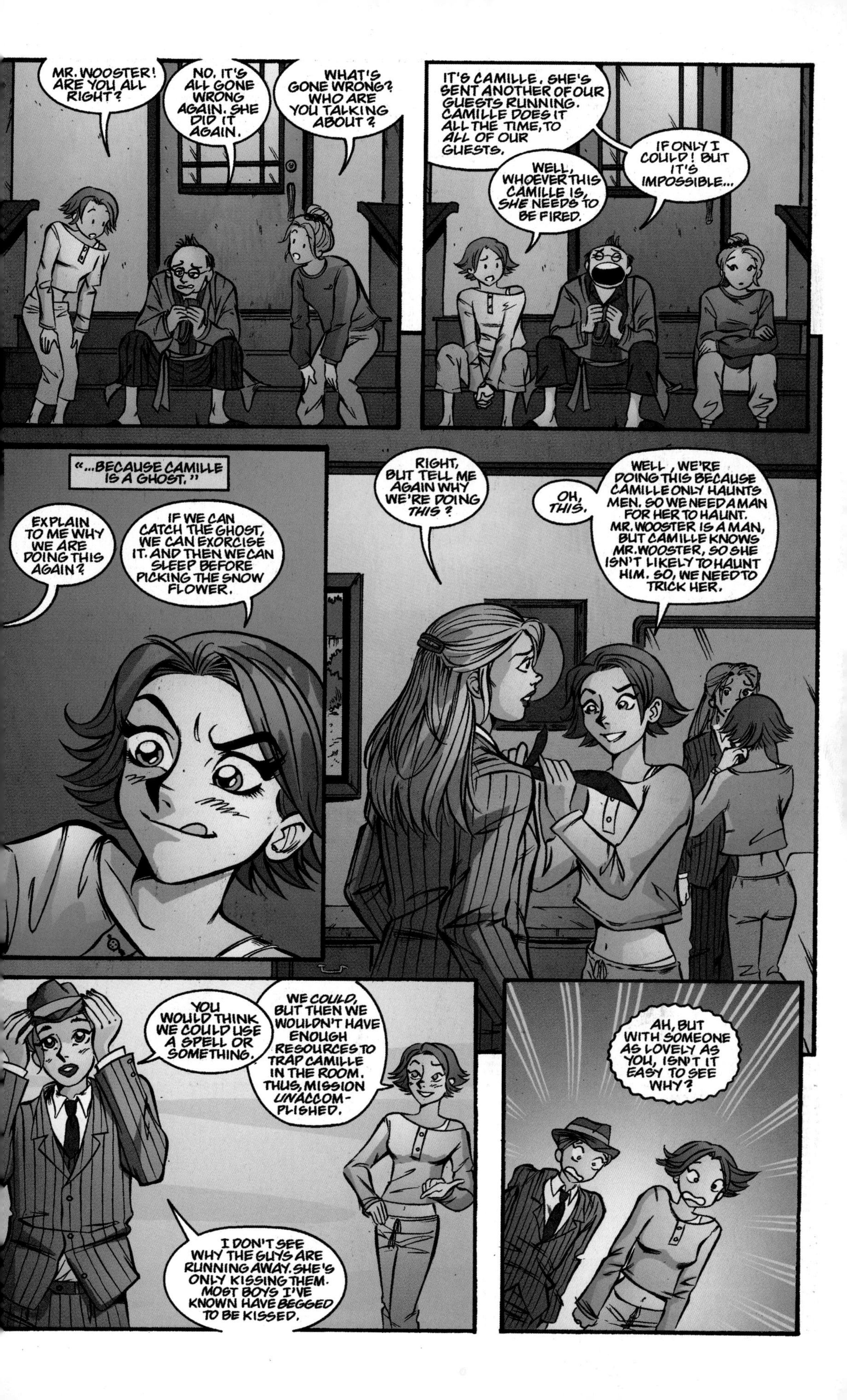
MR. WOOSTER! ARE YOU ALL RIGHT?
NO, IT'S ALL GONE WRONG AGAIN. SHE DID IT AGAIN.
WHAT'S GONE WRONG? WHO ARE YOU TALKING ABOUT?
IT'S CAMILLE. SHE'S SENT ANOTHER OF OUR GUESTS RUNNING. CAMILLE DOES IT ALL THE TIME, TO ALL OF OUR GUESTS.
WELL, WHOEVER THIS CAMILLE IS, SHE NEEDS TO BE FIRED.
IF ONLY I COULD! BUT IT'S IMPOSSIBLE...
"...BECAUSE CAMILLE IS A GHOST."
EXPLAIN TO ME WHY WE ARE DOING THIS AGAIN?
IF WE CAN CATCH THE GHOST, WE CAN EXORCISE IT. AND THEN WE CAN SLEEP BEFORE PICKING THE SNOW FLOWER.
RIGHT, BUT TELL ME AGAIN WHY WE'RE DOING THIS?
OH, THIS.
WELL, WE'RE DOING THIS BECAUSE CAMILLE ONLY HAUNTS MEN. SO WE NEED A MAN FOR HER TO HAUNT. MR. WOOSTER IS A MAN, BUT CAMILLE KNOWS MR. WOOSTER, SO SHE ISN'T LIKELY TO HAUNT HIM. SO, WE NEED TO TRICK HER.
YOU WOULD THINK WE COULD USE A SPELL OR SOMETHING.
WE COULD, BUT THEN WE WOULDN'T HAVE ENOUGH RESOURCES TO TRAP CAMILLE IN THE ROOM. THUS, MISSION UNACCOMPLISHED.
I DON'T SEE WHY THE GUYS ARE RUNNING AWAY. SHE'S ONLY KISSING THEM. MOST BOYS I'VE KNOWN HAVE BEGGED TO BE KISSED.
AH, BUT WITH SOMEONE AS LOVELY AS YOU, ISN'T IT EASY TO SEE WHY?

I MUST SAY, I'M NOT SURE IF I UNDERSTAND THE WAY YOU MODERN GIRLS LIKE TO DRESS, BUT THAT DOESN'T MEAN I DON'T LIKE IT.
UH-OH. I THINK MY CROSS-DRESSING ATTRACTED THE WRONG KIND OF GHOST.
THIS DOESN'T MAKE ANY SENSE...
...BUT I THINK IT'S BEST IF WE STICK TO THE PLAN.
WHAT HAVE YOU DONE?
OKAY, YOU... YOU... WHATEVER KIND OF GHOSTY THING YOU ARE! START TALKING!
YEAH! WHY AREN'T YOU CAMILLE?
CAMILLE? SHE'S MY WIFE! IS SHE WHO YOUR TRAP WAS FOR?
DON'T WORRY. ONCE SHE DISCOVERS I'M WITH YOU, SHE'LL BE ALONG SHORTLY. IN FACT...
OGGGDENN
...HERE SHE IS!
I SHOULD HAVE KNOWN YOU'D BE CHASING THE FIRST STRUMPETS THAT STEPPED THROUGH THAT DOOR.
HOWEVER ODDLY DRESSED THEY MAY BE.
BUT, MY BELOVED, ALL IS NOT AS IT SEEMS. I HAVE BEEN TRICKED AND TRAPPED...
... AS HAVE YOU.
YOU KNOW, IF YOU'D JUST GONE TO REST PEACEFULLY, WE WOULDN'T BE HERE.
ME?!?! SHALL I TELL THESE GIRLS WHAT YOU DID?
WE DON'T CARE WHAT HE DID...

"OH, BUT YOU SHOULD CARE. ALL MEN ARE DOGS. YOU DON'T THINK SO AT FIRST. I DIDN'T.
"WE CAME HERE ON OUR TENTH WEDDING ANNIVERSARY, AND I WAS STILL SO IN LOVE.
"BUT THEN THE INGENUE ENTERED AND EVERYTHING CHANGED. I SAW MY DEAR DOG OGDEN'S TRUE NATURE.
"I SWORE I'D HAVE REVENGE, HUMILIATE HIM IN THE VERY SPOT WHERE HE HUMILIATED ME.
"NO MATTER HOW LONG IT TOOK.
"WE DIED TOGETHER ON OUR TRIP HOME. WE WERE ARGUING, NOT WATCHING WHERE WE WERE GOING.
"I CAME BACK HERE, AND I'VE BEEN HUMILIATING HIM EVER SINCE, IN THE HOPES THAT HE'LL FEEL THE BURN OF BETRAYAL THAT I ONCE FELT."
LIES! I NEVER DID ANYTHING WITH THAT GIRL!
AND IF YOU WEREN'T SUCH A NAG, WE WOULDN'T HAVE TUMBLED TO OUR EARLY GRAVES!
OH, PLEASE.
SHUT UP!
NO WONDER MR. WOOSTER CAN'T KEEP ANY GUESTS! YOU TWO ARE LEAVING HERE, AND YOU'RE DOING IT TODAY!
FINE WITH US!

BANISHINGS... BANISHINGS... HERE WE GO!
OH, NO... THIS COULD BE A PROBLEM.
WHAT COULD BE A PROBLEM?
WELL, NOT A PROBLEM EXACTLY. WE JUST, UH, HAVE TO EXORCISE ONE SPIRIT AT A TIME. WHO WANTS TO GO FIRST?
OOOH, NO YOU DON'T!
I KNOW WHAT YOU'RE UP TO!
HE'S CONVINCED YOU ALL TO GET RID OF ME SO HE CAN COZY UP WITH THAT YOUNG TRAMP.
DO US A FAVOR. SHOW YOUR WIFE YOU AREN'T PLOTTING AGAINST HER BY GOING FIRST?
CERTAINLY NOT! I AM SICK OF UNFOUNDED ACCUSATIONS!
I SAW YOU WITH HER!
I NEVER DID ANYTHING, YOU HARPY!
WHOMP
WHOMP
WHOMP

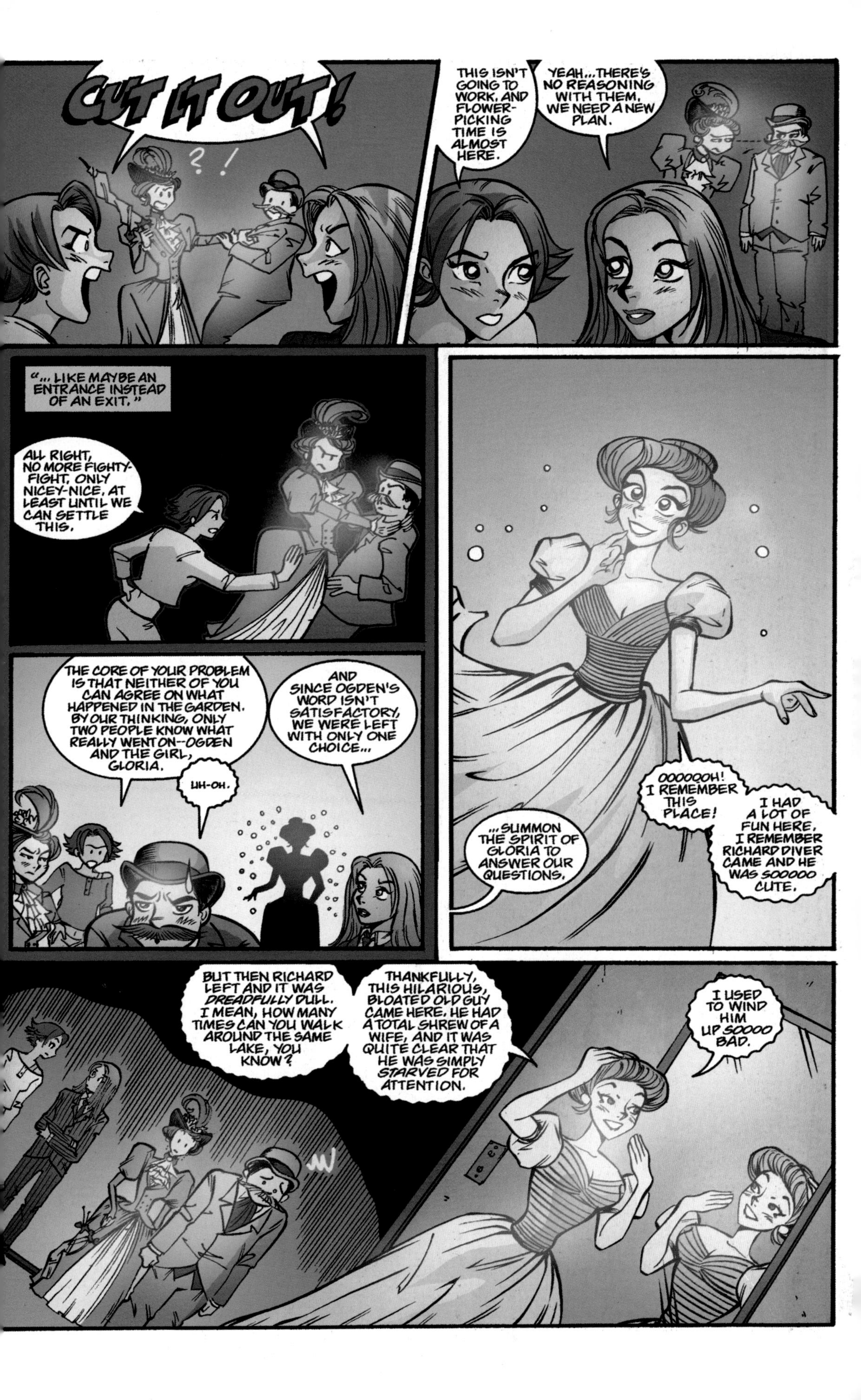
CUT IT OUT!
?!
THIS ISN'T GOING TO WORK, AND FLOWER-PICKING TIME IS ALMOST HERE.
YEAH...THERE'S NO REASONING WITH THEM. WE NEED A NEW PLAN.
"...LIKE MAYBE AN ENTRANCE INSTEAD OF AN EXIT."
ALL RIGHT, NO MORE FIGHTY-FIGHT, ONLY NICEY-NICE, AT LEAST UNTIL WE CAN SETTLE THIS.
THE CORE OF YOUR PROBLEM IS THAT NEITHER OF YOU CAN AGREE ON WHAT HAPPENED IN THE GARDEN. BY OUR THINKING, ONLY TWO PEOPLE KNOW WHAT REALLY WENT ON--OGDEN AND THE GIRL, GLORIA.
UH-OH.
AND SINCE OGDEN'S WORD ISN'T SATISFACTORY, WE WERE LEFT WITH ONLY ONE CHOICE...
...SUMMON THE SPIRIT OF GLORIA TO ANSWER OUR QUESTIONS.
OOOOOOH! I REMEMBER THIS PLACE!
I HAD A LOT OF FUN HERE. I REMEMBER RICHARD DIVER CAME AND HE WAS SOOOOO CUTE.
BUT THEN RICHARD LEFT AND IT WAS DREADFULLY DULL. I MEAN, HOW MANY TIMES CAN YOU WALK AROUND THE SAME LAKE, YOU KNOW?
THANKFULLY, THIS HILARIOUS, BLOATED OLD GUY CAME HERE. HE HAD A TOTAL SHREW OF A WIFE, AND IT WAS QUITE CLEAR THAT HE WAS SIMPLY STARVED FOR ATTENTION.
I USED TO WIND HIM UP SOOOO BAD.

WHAT WAS HIS NAME? OGLE? OBOE? OKAPI?
OH, GOD, IT'S TRUE! SHE TREATED ME HORRIBLY!
THE ONLY PART THAT WAS REMOTELY FLATTERING WAS HOW CAMILLE GOT SO UPSET. I LIKED THAT SHE THOUGHT A YOUNG GIRL WOULD WANT ME.
I'M SUCH A FOOL.
OH, OGGY....
I'M SO SORRY, CAMMY.
NONSENSE. WHAT BETTER WAY TO KICK OFF AN ETERNAL ROMANCE THAN WITH A LITTLE UNHOLY FIRE?
OCHRE? OLLIE--?
ALL RIGHT, ENOUGH OUT OF YOU. YOU CAN GO HOME NOW. SHEESH.
AND SO...
GOOD-BYE, MY LOVE. SEE YOU ON THE OTHER SIDE.
IT WON'T BE SOON ENOUGH FOR ME, TURTLEDOVE!
DON'T FRET, DARLING. I AM ON MY WAY!
UGH, I THINK I LIKED THEM BETTER WHEN THEY WERE FIGHTING.
MAN OH MAN, THAT WAS TIRING.
TELL ME ABOUT IT. MR. WOOSTER BETTER AT LEAST GIVE US A CUT RATE ON THE ROOM.
WHEN DO WE NEED TO GO PICK THE SNOW FLOWER?
IN AN HOUR, OR WAIT UNTIL NEXT YEAR.
NEXT YEAR IT IS.
GOOD PLAN.
THE END

Art by cliff Richards *with* p. craig Russell *and* Dave stewart

ONE SMALL PROMISE

One Small Promise
YOU SURE TIP WELL, BIG SPENDER.
WHAT CAN I SAY? DINNER WITH A PRETTY LADY ALWAYS MAKES ME FEEL GENEROUS.
FUNNY, I'M FEELING A LITTLE GENEROUS MYSELF.
A NECKLACE. WOW.
IT'S PURE SILVER.
YOU DON'T LIKE IT, DO YOU?
WHAT? OF COURSE I LIKE IT.

YOU REALLY THINK I'M GOING TO BUY THAT? I KNOW YOU WELL ENOUGH TO KNOW WHEN YOU'RE NOT TELLING ME SOMETHING.
I DON'T THINK THIS HAS EVER HAPPENED BEFORE. HOLD ON, LET ME THINK--
--NOPE. THIS IS TOTALLY NEW. I'VE NEVER HAD A WOMEN GIVE ME JEWELRY BEFORE.
SO, DOES THAT MEAN YOU DON'T LIKE IT OR WHAT?
COME ON, BUFFY! IT DOESN'T MEAN THAT AT ALL
COULD YOU TELL ME WHAT IT DOES MEAN, THEN?
WELL, WELL.
LOOKS LIKE WE'VE GOT A LONELY PAIR OF LOVERS, ALL READY FOR A NICE BITE.
CR.

IT MEANS... IT DOESN'T MEAN ANY-THING!
Uh-huh. THEN WHY AREN'T YOU PUTTING IT ON?
OKAY, OKAY. HERE'S ME... PUTTING ON MY NECKLACE.
OH, PLEASE. DON'T PATRONIZE ME.
EXCUSE ME, WE'RE ATTACKING YOU...
PATRONIZE?
YOU VAMPIRES ARE SO ALIKE-- RUN! SCREAM! BE SCARED! CAN'T YOU SEE WE'RE HAVING A MOMENT HERE? AT LEAST WE WERE UNTIL ONE OF US DECIDED TO GET ALL UNGRATE-FUL ON ME.

UNGRATEFUL? BUFFY, THAT'S NOT FAIR--
--HEY! I'M IN THE MIDDLE OF SOMETHING, HERE!
SO NOW I'M JUST "SOME THING"?
BUFFY, THAT'S LUDICROUS! WOULD YOU QUIT WITH THE SENSITIVE ROUTINE?
ARGH!

LUDICROUS?! ***SENSITIVE?*** OOOOOH, YOU ARE IN SOOO MUCH TROUBLE.
HEY, FLOSS YOUR OWN ICE! THAT BELONGS TO MY BOYFRIEND!

PUNCH
PUNCH
PUNCH
THANK YOU.

YOU KNOW I THINK YOU'RE THE GREATEST, RILEY, SO PLEASE, BE HONEST WITH ME. YOU WON'T HURT MY FEELINGS IF YOU'RE HONEST.
FAIR ENOUGH. BUT COULD YOU MAKE ME ONE SMALL PROMISE?

LET'S NEVER FIGHT AGAIN.
GUCCY
THE END
awwwww..

Art by Cliff Richards *with* Will Conrad *and* Dan Jackson

CITY OF DESPAIR

BUT I CAN BE READY IN FIVE MINUTES.
GOOD FOR YOU, BUT YOU STILL CAN'T COME.
YOU'RE NOT REALLY BEING FAIR ABOUT THIS, BUFFY.
RILEY, LISTEN TO ME. THERE'S SO MUCH GOING ON RIGHT NOW...
I KNOW, I'M SORT OF IN THE MIDDLE OF IT.
...AND I REALLY DON'T HAVE TIME FOR THIS TONIGHT.
WHOA! SO I'M ONLY GOOD FOR ONE THING, HUH?
RILEY FINN! THAT'S NOT WHAT I MEAN, AND YOU KNOW IT.
ACTUALLY...
THIS IS EXACTLY WHY I DON'T WANT YOU THERE.
THERE'LL BE TIME FOR THIS LATER, BUT RIGHT NOW WITH EVERYTHING THE WAY IT IS... I CAN'T DEAL.
UC SUNNYDALE
DON'T BE MAD AT ME FOR TRYING TO LOOK OUT FOR YOU--

ALL RIGHT, WHO'S NEXT?

THANKS FOR DINNER, MOM, BUT I'VE GOT TO GO.
WELL, I'M JUST GLAD YOU COULD MAKE IT DOWN, AT LEAST FOR A LITTLE BIT.
I--I STILL WISH WE HAD MORE TIMES LIKE THESE.
MOM! PLEASE...
I'M SORRY, I KNOW YOU'RE BUSY WITH SCHOOL AND EVERY-THING...
...BUT A MOTHER GETS CONCERNED.
MOSTLY THAT EVERY-THING PART.
SOMETIMES I S HERE ALONE A CAN'T HELP WONDERING: DO YOU HAVE EVER THING YOU NEED? ARE YO EATING ENOUGH?
ARE YOU DATING?
MOM, I'VE *REALLY* GOT TO GO.
OKAY, I GET THE HINT. JUST REMEMBER--

"--I'M ALWAYS HERE IF YOU WANT TO TALK."

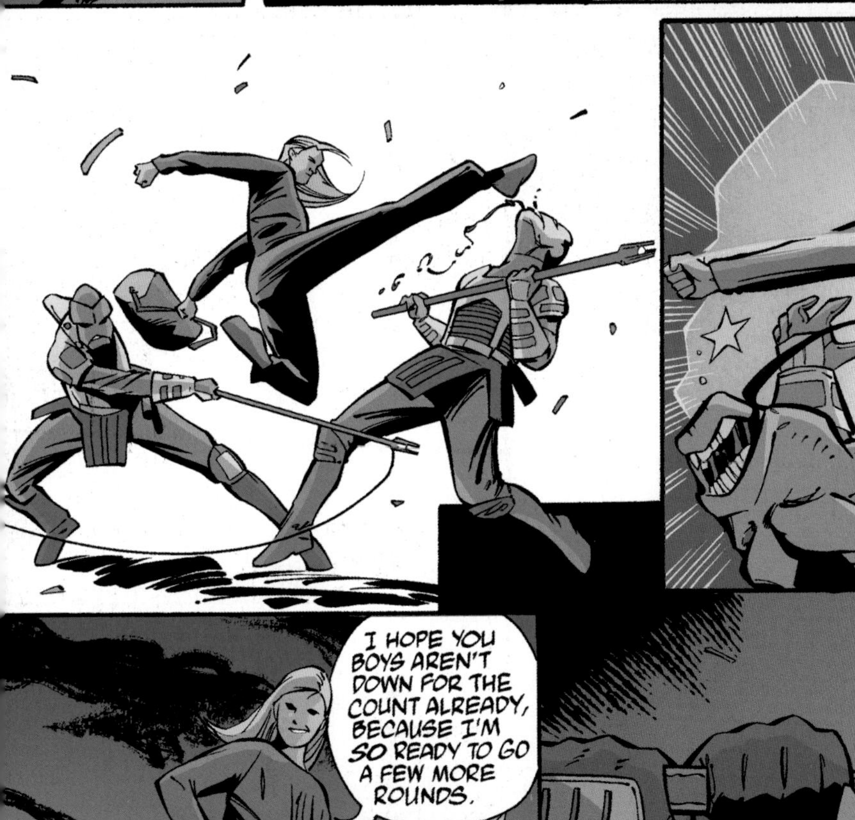

I HOPE YOU BOYS AREN'T DOWN FOR THE COUNT ALREADY, BECAUSE I'M *SO* READY TO GO A FEW MORE ROUNDS.

SSLOOSH!
ANOTHER VICTORY FOR YOU, FATHER. SOON I'LL BE FREE.

HOW CAN YOU RESIST THE POWER OF THIS PLACE?
YOU'RE ALWAYS FILLED WITH DIGNITY AND HONOR--EVEN WHEN FIGHTING UNDER THE STARE OF ALL THOSE EYES...
EVERY TIME I'M VICTORIOUS, I KNOW I'M ONE STEP CLOSER TO FREEDOM. THAT'S MY STRENGTH.
ONLY FOR THOSE WHO ARE WEAK.
BAH! THAT'S MAGIC POISONING YOUR MIND. THERE'S NO FREEDOM HERE, ONLY DEATH.
HEY! WATCH THOSE HANDS!
ANGEL?
WELL, WELL. JUST LIKE OLD TIMES.

YEAH, BUT LET'S CATCH UP LATER. YOU WANT TO HELP ME FIGURE OUT WHERE IN THE HELL WE ARE?
OKAY, THEN, WE'LL GET DOWN TO BUSINESS. THIS ISN'T HELL, BUT I DON'T THINK IT'S EARTH EITHER. LOOK OUT THERE...
GLADIATORS? I HEAR THEY'RE ALL THE RAGE.
I GOT CAUGHT UP IN SOMETHING LIKE THIS BACK IN L.A., BUT NOWHERE NEAR THIS...ELABORATE.
YOU'D BETTER LIKE TO FIGHT. EVERYONE FIGHTS HERE-- LONELINESS, DESPAIR, BOREDOM. THERE'S NO ESCAPING IT.
UGH. NICE BREATH. BRUSH MUCH?
IT CAN'T BE... THE CITY OF DESPAIR. I ALWAYS THOUGHT IT WAS A FABLE.
I'VE HEARD THAT BEFORE. THIS FABLE GIVE YOU ANY HINTS ON HOW WE GET OUT?
NOT REALLY. THE LEGEND SAYS A RACE OF DEMONS, THE GEFA'AR, SEARCH THE KNOWN WORLDS AND ABDUCT THE BEST FIGHTERS TO COMPETE FOR THEIR ENTERTAINMENT. AS THE STORY GOES, ONCE YOU'VE BEEN CAPTURED, THERE'S NO WAY BACK.
ARRGHHH

SHE WON'T RESPOND AT ALL. NOT TO BE ALL OBVIOUS, BUT I THINK THIS NECK-BAND THINGIE IS THE CAUSE.
I WOULDN'T MESS WITH IT. DEFINITELY DEMONIC IN DESIGN.
AGREED. APPARENTLY IT'S SOME-THING USED BY...
...THE BLUE GEFA'AR. WE WOULDN'T HAVE MUCH LUCK REMOVING IT.
WELL, WE'D BETTER FIGURE OUT HOW TO GET IT OFF--AND FAST. HE'S GETTING WORSE.
GOOD NIGHT, GOLIATH.

QUITE THE PERFORMANCE. BEEN WATCHING THE *WWF*?
SOMETHING THE NEW BOY-FRIEND IS INTO?
THAT'S NONE OF YOUR BUSINESS. LET'S STICK TO THE HERE AND NOW, PLEASE.
FINE.
WHAT WAS IT LIKE OUT THERE?
STRANGE... MY MIND WAS CLEAR, BUT IT FELT LIKE SOME-THING WAS CONTROLLING ME. I HAD TO *FIGHT* TO PLEASE THE CROWD.
WHAT YOU FELT WAS THE POWER OF THE COLLAR. IN THE RING, IT FEEDS ON YOUR ANGER AND GUILT. IN HERE, IT SAPS YOUR WILL. DO NOT LET IT BREAK YOUR SPIRIT. FIGHT IT!
LOOKS TO ME LIKE YOU'RE NO BETTER OFF THAN WE ARE.
WHY IS EVERYONE GOING ALL OBI-WAN HERE? WE NEED TO DO SOME-THING...
BUT I AM KOR! AND I'M CLOSE TO BREAKING THE GEFA'AR'S MAGIC.
AND YOU'VE BEEN WORKING ON THIS PLAN HOW LONG?
LONG ENOUGH TO KNOW THAT FOR EACH FIGHT-ER WHO TRULY WIELDS HOPE, THAT'S ONE MORE WHO CAN CARVE THE PATH TO FREEDOM.
RELYING ON HOPE AND FAITH ISN'T MUCH OF A PLAN.
I SEE I CAN'T COUNT ON YOUR FRIEND TO HELP. WHAT ABOUT YOU?
ALL I KNOW IS THAT I'VE GOT TOO MUCH TO WORRY ABOUT IN MY OWN LIFE TO DEAL WITH BEING HERE.

OOOF!
OOWWOOWW!

FATHER, I CAN'T FEEL YOU! WHERE HAVE YOU GONE?
VTTTT!

LOOK WHERE HIS PLAN GOT HIM.
MAYBE HE WAS RIGHT. HE TALKED ABOUT BREAKING THE MAGIC... THERE'S GOT TO BE A SIMPLE WAY TO GET HOME.
THEN WHAT IS IT? NOW YOU'VE GOT THE ANSWERS?
I'M NOT ANY HAPPIER TO BE HERE THAN YOU, BUT IT'S TIME TO PULL TOGETHER, NOT POUT.
THE MORE I STRUGGLE AGAINST THIS COLLAR, THE MORE IT SAPS MY ENERGY. CAN'T YOU FEEL THAT?
YES, AND IT SUCKS. BUT I WON'T DIE HERE, NO MATTER WHAT.
OF COURSE! THE CITY OF DESPAIR RESIDES ON THE ASTRAL PLANE, AND THAT'S WHERE ANGEL AND BUFFY'S ASTRAL ESSENCES ARE AS WELL. AND THESE COLLARS...
...HOLD THEM THERE. WE'VE GOT TO FIGURE OUT HOW TO REMOVE THEM. I FEAR SOMETHING DREADFUL IS ABOUT TO HAPPEN.

I DON'T WANT TO DO THIS.
IT DOESN'T SEEM WE HA A CHOICE
UNGH!
I... CAN'T... FIGHT IT.
I DON'T KNOW MUCH LONGER I CAN RESIST.
NOT LONG ENOUGH--
I'M THROUG WITH THIS.

ANGEL, PLEASE! I DON'T WANT TO FIGHT WITH YOU ANYMORE!
YOU THINK I'M ENJOYING THIS?!
NOT ANY MORE THAN ME! BUT I'VE FIGURED OUT WHAT'S KEEPING US TRAPPED HERE!
WE ALREADY KNOW IT'S THE COLLARS!
NO, IT'S OUR OWN DESPAIR. COME HERE. HUG ME.
BUT...
YOU GOTTA TRUST ME.

WMMMM
ANGEL!
OH, MAN.
ARE YOU OKAY? WE WERE, LIKE, SOOO WORRIED. WEREN'T WE, WESLEY?
WESLEY?
YOU WERE IN THE CITY OF DESPAIR, WEREN'T YOU?
YES. IT FEELS LIKE...A DREAM.
AND YOU ESCAPED. I DON'T THINK THAT'S EVER BEEN DONE BEFORE. HOW IN THE WORLD DID YOU MANAGE IT?
...AND THAT'S ALL IT TOOK.
YOU CAN'T SERIOUSLY EXPECT ME TO BELIEVE THAT A SIMPLE HUG...
YOU CAN'T UNDERESTIMATE THE POWER OF GOOD HUGGING.
EVEN WITH ANGEL?
MOM, I'M GLAD YOU'RE HERE.
WHERE ELSE WOULD I BE? I WAS CONCERNED. YOU CAN'T BLAME A MOTHER FOR BEING CONCERNED--
LISTEN, OUR LAST DINNER WAS TOO SHORT. LET'S DO IT AGAIN. THIS TIME I'VE GOT SOMEONE I'D LIKE YOU TO MEET.
THE END

Art by Christian Zanier with Guy Major

LOOK FOR THESE BUFFY THE VAMPIRE SLAYER TRADE PAPERBACKS FROM TITAN BOOKS.

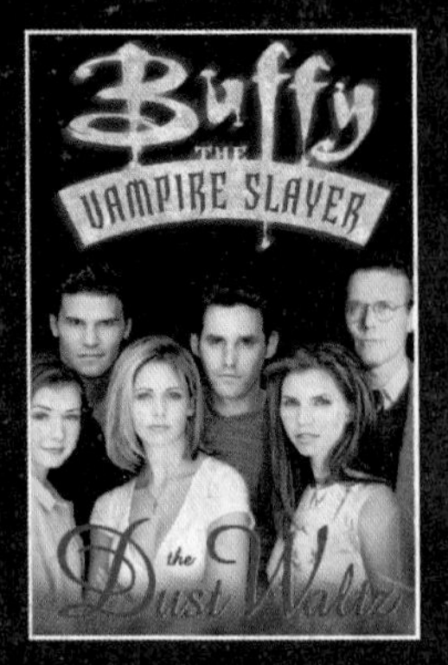

The Dust Waltz
Brereton • Gomez • Florea
80-page color paperback
ISBN: 1-84023-057-6 **£7.99**

The Remaining Sunlight
Watson • Bennett • Ketcham
80-page color trde paperback
ISBN: 1-84023-078-9 **£7.99**

The Origin
Golden • Brereton • Bennett • Ketcham
80-page color paperback
ISBN: 1-84023-105-X **£7.99**

Uninvited Guests
Watson • Gomez • Florea
104-page color paperback
ISBN: 1-84023-140-8 **£8.99**

Supernatural Defense Kit
Watson • Richards • Pimentel
30-page color hard cover
comes with golden-colored cross,
"claddagh" ring, and vial of "Holy water"
ISBN: 1-84023-165-3 **£19.99**

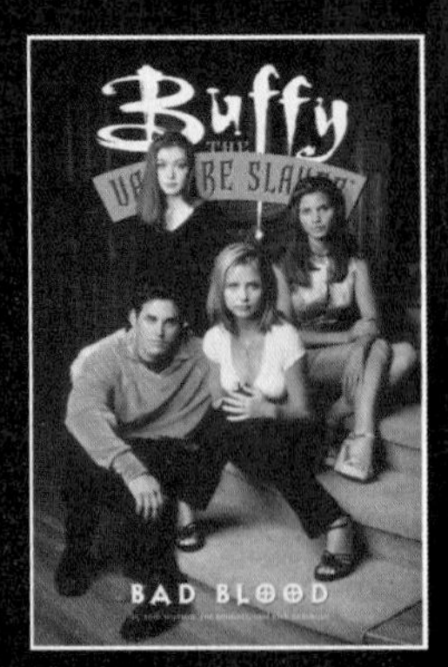

Bad Blood
Watson • Bennett • Ketcham
88-page color paperback
ISBN: 1-84023-179-3 **£8.99**

Crash Test Demons
Watson • Richards • Pimentel
88-page color paperback
ISBN: 1-84023-199-8 **£8.99**

Angel: The Hollower
Golden • Gomez • Florea
88-page color paperback
ISBN: 1-84023-163-7 **£8.99**

Coming Soon!
Ring of Fire
Petrie • Sook
80-page color paperback
ISBN: 1-84023-200-5

www.buffy.com

All publications are available through most good bookshops or dire from our mail order service at Titan Books. For a free graphic-nove catalogue or to order, telephone 01858 433 169 with your credit-card deta or contact Titan Books Mail Order, Bowden House, 36 Northampton Ro Market Harborough, Leics, LE16 9HE, quoting reference BFC/GN